THE
KING'S
HORRIBLE
BRIDE

THE KING'S HORRIBLE BRIDE

First Edition: May 2018
Second Edition: May 2020
www.katiwilde.com

ALSO BY KATI WILDE

The Hellfire Riders Series

THE HELLFIRE RIDERS: SAXON & JENNY
THE HELLFIRE RIDERS: JACK & LILY
BREAKING IT ALL
GIVING IT ALL
CRAVING IT ALL
FAKING IT ALL
LOSING IT ALL

Contemporary Romance

GOING NOWHERE FAST
SECRET SANTA
ALL HE WANTS FOR CHRISTMAS
THE KING'S HORRIBLE BRIDE
THE WEDDING NIGHT

The Dead Lands

THE MIDWINTER MAIL-ORDER BRIDE
PRETTY BRIDE
THE MIDNIGHT BRIDE

Wolfkin & Berserkers

BEAUTY IN SPRING
HIGH MOON
TEACHER'S PET WOLF

THE ROYAL WEDDING SERIES

The King's Spinster Bride by Ruby Dixon

The King's Horrible Bride by Kati Wilde

The King's Innocent Bride by Alexa Riley

The King's Reluctant Bride by Ella Goode

THE KING'S HORRIBLE BRIDE

KATI WILDE

Mad Maximilian

—From the feature article "Mad Maximilian" in
VANITY FAIR, May 2018

Nestled between the borders of Switzerland *and Austria lies the small Alpine kingdom of Kapria. You probably haven't heard of it; few people born outside the region know it even exists. Although the Kingdom of Kapria was established in 1465 and its monarchy has long declared that Kapria is a sovereign state, it has not been formally recognized by many other European nations. And although its physical territory is slightly larger in area than the better-known microstate to the north, Liechtenstein, many atlases don't even draw in the kingdom's political boundaries. Consult any*

GPS system while in the kingdom, and it will claim you are still in Switzerland—and a traveler watching through the windows of a train or automobile might not even recognize that they've left that country while passing through Kapria's small capital city or its collection of quaint villages.

Now one man is—quite literally—putting his kingdom on the map.

King Maximilian was only twenty years old when he ascended to Kapria's troubled throne. Following an unmemorable coronation ceremony (the depleted treasury couldn't support a lavish affair—not that the kingdom's debt had ever stopped his father's extravagant spending), the young king blistered his father's memory in a rousing speech, seething with rage at how his country had faltered under King Leopold's corrupt rule, and promising that he would not rest until every Kaprian had a better future in sight.

For a moment, Kapria gained the world's attention—and Maximilian earned the world's ridicule, his speech dismissed as the ravings of an immature, naive ruler. After all, an impoverished nation cannot pull itself up by its bootstraps when it is treading on bare feet.

And maybe it never would have, if the billionaire Wilhelm Dietrich hadn't given Kapria's new king a pair of golden boots.

Before Wilhelm, the Dietrichs were a noble family of little consequence and only notable for a history of mild eccentricity. The family had been centered in the Kaprian village of Gentian until King Leopold came into power. To escape that king's tyrannical regime, a young Wilhelm fled with his parents

THE KING'S HORRIBLE BRIDE

to Switzerland, and over the following decades established himself as a giant of industry and finance.

Then, twelve years ago—whether inspired by Maximilian's coronation speech or simply just as eccentric as his ancestors—the multi-billionaire transferred nearly the entirety of his assets to the young king, instantly making him the richest man in Europe. With the influx of wealth into his country's coffers, Maximilian began restoring his kingdom's infrastructure and implementing new social programs.

He spent Dietrich's money well. Today Kapria boasts the lowest unemployment rate in the world, even among the refugee population. It has the lowest poverty rate in the world, the lowest incarceration rate, and one of the lowest tax rates.

It also has the highest graduation rate—and a government willing to pay for vocational school or four-year university after graduation—and a robust apprenticeship culture. Citizens enjoy free electricity and internet access, along with free public transportation and healthcare.

But all of these improvements weren't merely the result of a monetary donation. Because among his other assets, Wilhelm Dietrich gave to Kapria's king something far more valuable than gold: one of his own inventions, the Vic-10 reactor. The clean, stable, super-efficient reactor uses a saltwater solution as fuel, and is powerful enough that a midsize family car can run for twenty thousand miles on a single gallon of water.

That's not a typo. Twenty thousand miles. A single gallon of water.

The reactor is already in use in Kapria's newly built

power plant, which supplies the entire kingdom's electricity at a minuscule cost. A negative cost, in truth, because they sell the excess power to Switzerland, one of the few nations that already recognizes Kapria's sovereignty.

But the number of nations is set to increase dramatically.

Today, the first time I see King Maximilian in person, I'm crowded together with dozens of journalists. We're escorted into his throne room, where he'll sign the trade agreement that will license the reactor technology to countries that have suddenly become very interested in officially recognizing this small kingdom. Publicity photos often show Maximilian in a suit and tie, or with his shirtsleeves rolled up and intently at work. Now he wears a formal uniform reminiscent of military design. His dark hair is cropped close to his scalp, as austere as it was during his service in Kapria's small militia. He cuts an imposing figure in both height and breadth, but the seething anger of the young king has cooled and sharpened. If he had been more inclined to follow in his father's hedonistic footsteps, his starkly handsome features would have been the darling of every tabloid and gossip rag, but those publications are more likely to capture the king's forbidding scowl than catch him in a scandal. Despite the severity of his appearance, he's not known for harshness or cruelty. Over the course of the past decade he's built a reputation as a fair and just ruler, and one who is utterly dedicated to the advancement of his kingdom.

In that goal, he has wildly succeeded. Today, few people know Maximilian's name or Kapria's location. Tomorrow, he will be known as the monarch who dragged a failing European *kingdom into the 21st century…and who might have solved the world's energy crisis while he did.*

The reverent silence that fills his office chambers when Maximilian picks up his gold fountain pen vanishes the moment he begins scrawling his signature across the bottom of the trade agreement. A burst of camera flashes and clicking shutters surround him like a flock of vultures during a lightning storm.

That storm abates as he signs the duplicate documents, then renews as he rises from his desk to shake the hands of foreign politicians and diplomats, all of them beaming with their congratulations and their satisfaction in the agreement.

As Maximilian poses with each foreign dignitary for the cameras, his rare smile appears more often than it usually does—perhaps because their money will soon flood into his kingdom and wash away the remaining stench of his father's unprincipled reign. For twelve years, from the moment King Leopold dropped dead of an embolism, Maximilian has labored to repair the damage his father had wrought to the country. Twelve years of small, determined steps. But today's trade agreement signifies a giant leap forward for Kapria, and fulfills a promise he made to his people on the day he ascended to the throne.

So perhaps for the first time in a very long time, King Maximilian has something to smile about.

Victoria

"Holy shit." My sister flattens her hand over her heart and staggers back, her gaze fixed on the television screen, where Kapria's public broadcasting network is documenting the signing ceremony in the palace's throne room. "He's smiling. King Maximilian is smiling! Do you think he's possessed by demons?"

More likely, he exorcised a few of his demons when he signed the trade agreement. But I know better than to encourage Liz's dramatics. If I play along, within a few minutes she'll be dressing up in horns and a tail, then find a pitchfork that she'll use to exorcise *my* demons.

Besides, I can't stop looking at Maximilian's smile.

I've seen thousands of photos and watched hundreds of hours of video footage featuring Kapria's king, and this is the first time that particular smile has ever appeared: broad, genuine. Beautiful.

He's beautiful when he's not smiling, too—but in an intense, razor-edged way. I've never seen him so…at ease.

Already bored by the public broadcast, Liz sidles closer to the sofa where I'm sitting—and closer to the lunch of cheese and fruit that I've placed on the table beside me. Without taking my gaze from the screen, I reach for the two fat strawberries that I'm saving for my dessert, lick them both, and put them back down.

"Damn it," she pouts. "You can't share?"

"You can't get your own?" I retort. "There's more in the kitchen."

"They taste better when they're stolen. But not when they're contaminated with your germs." She feigns a horrified shudder. "A *good* sister would share."

"Mmm-hmm," I agree. "But I'm not."

Though I am. And we both know it. So she narrows her green eyes at me in mock anger and threatens, "You're going to regret this," before flouncing from the conservatory with her long auburn ponytail swinging behind her.

I probably *will* regret it. No doubt I'll wake up with toothpaste in my hair or raw eggs in my running shoes. My little sister has more energy than a sack full of cats, but ever since she graduated from university last summer, she hasn't applied that energy toward anything. Before her graduation, our brother James—her twin—was at home during the same holidays that she was, so he was the focus of her attention. But with James serving two years as a volunteer in the Kaprian militia, she's dedicated her *many* free hours to—in her words—livening up my staid, boring life.

Maybe my life is a trifle staid, but that's the way I like it. And it's not boring. Not to me, at least. I can see why Liz thinks so, though. She's the kind of person who always needs to be entertained, so she bounces around until she finds something interesting to do or until someone provides that entertainment. But I don't need constant external stimulation. If nothing's happening around me, I'll still find ways to occupy myself.

But it's not often that nothing's happening around me. I'm always busy. Today is one of the rare days I have to myself, so I'm determined to do the things I love best. That's why I'm in the conservatory, relaxing in the sunshine streaming through the giant windows and watching the most beautiful man in the world smile as he secures Kapria's future.

"Vic!" Liz's shout echoes down the manor house's ancient halls. "Can I borrow your turquoise sweater?"

I'm not yelling my answer back. Instead I text her. *Yes.* I *can* share. Just not my strawberries.

Another shout rings out. "You're the best!"

I know. But when my gaze returns to the handsome, smiling face onscreen, I wonder if my best is good enough for a king.

My chest tightens. Twelve years have passed since
my father and the newly crowned Maximilian struck
the deal that would change his life—and mine—forever. At sixteen years of age, I was quietly betrothed to
a king. Two months ago, I celebrated my twenty-eighth
birthday. And so much time has passed without a single
word from Maximilian…maybe the king has changed
his mind. Maybe everything I've been working toward
and hoping for will never become a reality. Maybe he'll
want someone else. Someone he's met more than once.
Maybe he'll fall in love with them.

Maybe he's completely forgotten about me.

But I refuse to wallow in self-doubt—or self-pity.
Determinedly I push up out of the sofa, grab my lunch
plate, and head out to the garden. The early afternoon
sunlight is too harsh for my purposes, so I spend the next
hour leisurely searching for the perfect blooms before
returning to the house for my camera and tripod. By the
time the light has softened, I'm in position to capture a
cluster of alpine wildflowers. At my request, our gardener
has been carefully cultivating some of the endangered
species that grow in the higher elevations of the Kaprian
mountains. He once grumbled to me that a single garden
won't save the flowers, but saving them has never been
my intention. Not directly, anyway. Instead I'm hoping to
help raise awareness and capture the attention of nature
enthusiasts.

"Are you out here, Vic?" Liz yells.

This time I won't text the answer. Bent over the tripod, I call back, "By the north arbor!"

She shows up on the path a moment later, but she's not alone. A man I don't recognize strolls along behind her, his hands tucked casually in the pockets of his suit trousers.

Oh shit. I straighten, wishing she'd told me we have a guest. Then I could have sent her back into the house and changed my clothes before meeting him, instead of standing barefoot in the grass, wearing a pair of faded cutoffs and an ancient hooded sweatshirt. I have good reason to protect my image. I'm not always perfectly successful. I've had a few missteps, but those missteps were accidental. This could have been avoided if he'd been properly announced.

But Liz doesn't know about the betrothal. Not really. Before our father died, I often said the king had promised to marry me and that I would be Kapria's queen. But I haven't spoken of that agreement for years, so Liz and James—who are six years younger than I am—only remember my claims as a teenage crush and wishful thinking. They don't know why I protect my public face so fiercely. It's one of the things Liz teases me about—that I never leave the house with a hair out of place. Which isn't true. Not really. Sometimes the wind blows and I can't do anything to stop that, so I don't try. If I *can* control something, however, I will.

The only thing I can control now is my reaction to our unexpected visitor. In his mid-thirties, with dark blond hair and a medium height and build, he looks vaguely familiar in a nondescript way, but I can't place him. "Good afternoon, Mr…?"

"Karl Sauer." His gaze scans me from toes to head with a focus that's both disinterestedly nonthreatening and strangely invasive. As if he's measuring me with that one look but trying to appear as if he isn't. He glances at Liz before returning his attention to me. His accent is distinctly American when he says, "I am here to deliver a personal message from my employer. Can we speak privately?"

Liz's eyes flare wide. She purses her lips and shoots me a look brimming with irrepressible humor. As if she's waiting for the day's entertainment to begin.

Oh lord. I know that look all too well. Chances are, she's either setting me up for a date or this is part of a prank. I'm not sure which is worse.

But I'll play along for now. Lifting my chin, I say as regally as possible, "Liz, will you give Mr. Sauer and me a few moments of privacy?" *You little snot.*

"Sure," she replies, then mouths something that looks like *"ride that pony"* before skipping away.

As soon as she's out of sight, I ask Sauer, "And your employer is…?"

"Maximilian," he says bluntly. "Your king."

My heart thumps, hard. For a moment the edges of

my vision turn black as if the blood has drained from my head. Then my brain cells start working again.

If this man is an emissary of the king, then I'm a dancing ostrich. For one, he's American—and Maximilian makes a point of hiring Kaprian citizens. His staff includes some naturalized immigrants, but anyone who works for the king or in the palace has been tutored in etiquette and refers to him in a specific manner. They don't just say "Maximilian." Instead they refer to him as "His Majesty," or at least append his title to his name. And if this man were a Kaprian citizen, Maximilian wouldn't be "your king." He'd be "ours."

Maybe he's new to Kapria. And maybe he does work at the palace. But if he's a recent hire, would he be sent on this particular mission? No. Far more likely, this is Liz's work. And he does look somewhat familiar. Maybe he's an actor she hired. Or maybe I've seen him around the village or in the city, and Liz picked him up at a local café. With her, who knows.

But I'm particularly good at thinking one thing while emoting another. So I merely arch my eyebrows, indicating bland interest.

"Oh?" I question politely. "What message does he have for me?"

"That he wants to marry you."

His reply is a punch to the chest, but I conceal that, too. "All right. Tell him that I'll look for a clear space on my calendar," I say easily, then turn toward my camera, because I can only pretend so far. With throat aching, I tell him, "Now I hope you'll forgive me, but the sun keeps moving. If I don't take these photos at the right moment, the shadows will be all wrong."

From behind me comes a brief and palpably befuddled silence. Then, "You want me to tell the king that you'll look for a clear space on your calendar?"

"Mmm-hmmm," I hum the confirmation while I snap a few shots, then tug my phone out of my pocket and open the calendar app. "Let me see. It looks like…" I scroll through the months. And continue scrolling. "I have a few days free in October."

He nods sharply. "I will inform him—"

"October of next year, that is." With a shrug, I return to my camera. "I'm *so* very busy, after all. But I'm sure that His Majesty understands how it is, as he himself is so very busy that he could not even come here in person to announce our forthcoming wedding. Indeed, I'm *astonished* that he's had time to think of marriage at all, since he has been working obsessively for months to negotiate this trade agreement, and that was only signed an hour ago. Simply astonished!"

"As am I," Sauer says dryly, then offers a stiff bow. "Thank you for your time, my lady."

I'm not a lady. My father was a baron—and now my brother is—so I don't rate higher than a "miss" when someone addresses me. Someone who worked for the royal family would know that. And an emissary from the king would have been prepped before coming. Viciously I click the shutter again before smiling at him pleasantly. "You're welcome, Mr. Sauer. Don't forget to report to Liz and tell her how her little joke went."

He hesitates for a moment, as if about to say more, then shakes his head and departs.

I stand in place, the viewfinder blurry and unfocused through my tears. Liz couldn't know how this prank would hurt me. She teases me now and then about my girlhood crush on the king—and sometimes that teasing includes asking me if I never date because I'm still waiting for him to make me his queen. No doubt she believed I would be as unaffected by this joke as I am when she teases me.

Except I'm not unaffected, even by the teasing—I just pretend to be. And I *am* waiting for the king to make me his queen. Kind of. Because as the years pass, the possibility of marrying him seems to move further away, not closer. At eighteen, the reason for the delay was clear. My father had just succumbed to a brain tumor, and I was so young. At twenty-two, when I graduated from university, I was probably still too young—and Kapria was still recovering from King Leopold's rule. It made sense that Maximilian wouldn't want to indulge in an expensive wedding celebration while so many people in his kingdom were still struggling. And I don't expect a fairy tale where Maximilian shows up and sweeps me into his arms, declaring his passionate love. But a little acknowledgment would be nice. In all this time, I've only received one message from him—congratulations for earning my university degree. But I've done so much more since then. And although I understand all of the reasons for keeping the betrothal secret, I've moved from feeling as if he's being discreet… to feeling as if I'm invisible to him.

And I'm not too young to be queen now. Instead I worry that if he waits any longer, I won't be young *enough*.

Because I can't stop time any more than I can stop the wind. Or stop the Earth from turning. And while I'm wallowing in my hurt, the sun passes beyond the peaked roof of the manor house and the wildflowers fall into full shadow.

So much for waiting for the perfect moment.

But surely more than one perfect moment comes along in a lifetime. And it's not as if I can change the past now. I just have to move on.

I pick up my tripod and begin scouting for another spot—and wonder whether it's time to move on in other ways, too. Because I'm not Sleeping Beauty, untouched by time and unaware of its passing. I've been awake all these years, waiting for my king to arrive. But Maximilian hasn't shown any inclination to come.

So maybe I should tell him that he doesn't need to.

Maximilian

My cheeks ache from smiling. They genuinely fucking *ache*, the way my shoulders sometimes do after one of Karl's particularly grueling sparring sessions.

Who the hell would have thought that a face needed an exercise regimen?

The Minister of the Treasury's face is getting a workout, too, but the laugh lines etched deeply around Philippa's dark eyes prove it's one that she's accustomed to. Me, I'm just glad it's over. The gaggle of journalists and foreign dignitaries have been ushered from the throne room, leaving only the members of my ministerial cabinet and a bevy of assistants and palace staff.

With a grin, Philippa hands me a crystal snifter and pours in a measure of good Kaprian brandy. "You must feel as if the weight of the world just dropped off your shoulders."

I've never carried the weight of the world. Only the weight of a kingdom. And that burden only feels marginally lighter now. Licensing the reactor's technology will bring in a fortune to Kapria, but the licensing agreements have a fifty-year expiration date, and soon enough the world will have adapted and updated the Vic-10 far beyond its original design. So I have a single lifetime to make certain that Kapria becomes an economic and financial powerhouse, with enough stability to weather the eventual decline in foreign income. I won't leave the same mess to my children that my father left to me, and I refuse to let my people struggle and suffer as they did under his rule.

This was a significant milestone. But it's not the end of the journey. There's still much to do—beginning with my children. Because I don't have any. Yet.

But it's the next item on my agenda. One I'm eager to start.

Hopefully Victoria is ready, too.

I'll know soon if she is. I turn toward my assistant, seeking any news he might have received from Karl, but pause when Philippa's hand settles on my arm. A sudden silence falls over the throne room, and I realize each of the cabinet members are facing me with a drink in hand.

Solemnly, Frederich Groener lifts his into the air. "Raise

your glass to His Royal Majesty, who has dragged our fair kingdom out of the pit of social and economic ruin"—his lips twitch beneath his graying mustache—"despite the frequent kicking and screaming from the old guard."

Quite frequent. I chose each of my advisors partially because they openly opposed my father's policies, sometimes at a dear cost to themselves—but that doesn't mean they always support *my* policies. Or at least, not the way I go about implementing them. Our goals are often the same but my cabinet ministers almost always advise me to take small steps instead of giant leaps, and to be more restrained in my decisions.

They think I'm reckless. But I have no time for restraint. Not when the goal is improving the lives of my people.

"To Kapria," I reply, lifting my own glass. "May she ever shine bright."

"She'll shine brighter than the sun thanks to the Vic-10," my agricultural minister quips, drawing laughter from the others.

When it fades, Philippa adds softly, "And to Wilhelm Dietrich—may God rest his brilliant soul."

I'll happily drink to that. By handing over his fortune to Kapria's royal family, Wilhelm Dietrich gave the kingdom new hope for the future. In return, the dying billionaire only asked that his own family's future was secure and their legacy was preserved. I promised him that it would be, but that obligation is still unfulfilled.

Though not for much longer. Setting the snifter aside,

I glance at my assistant, Geoffrey, who might be the living embodiment of the Vic-10 reactor. He's small, efficient, possesses boundless energy—and, as far as I can tell, is fueled entirely by water. He's been with me for eight years and I've never seen him eat.

"In five minutes, you're scheduled to meet with Jeannette in your offices," Geoffrey immediately rattles off, "followed by an interview in the White Chamber with Andrew Bush from *Vanity Fair*. I've also arranged for tea in the south gardens a half hour into the interview. Since you're already decked out in the formal gear"—he waves his hand at me, indicating the uniform I'm wearing—"I told them they needed to complete the photo shoot today. And Jeannette confirmed with the magazine that you will be featured on the cover."

Good. This is a critical period. The Vic-10 has secured the world's attention. While we have that attention, we need to make the world look past the reactor to the kingdom itself. If that means plastering my face across a magazine—or fifty of them—I'll do it.

"Ask Frederich to join us in my offices," I tell Geoffrey, then offer Philippa the escort of my arm. "Let us go and further secure Kapria's future, madame."

"Maximilian." Her tone contains a gentle admonishment as her fingers curl around my proffered forearm. "You never rest. Will you not at least spend the remainder of the day celebrating your success?"

Celebration can come *after* the work is done. "On my

eighty-fifth birthday," I tell her. "I'll send up fireworks and watch them…for a few minutes."

If I don't waste those minutes before then. Simply shortening my stride to match Philippa's grandmotherly pace has me bursting with impatience. The few minutes that I promised to celebrate fifty-two years into the future feel as if they are being burned away as we slowly make our way down the long corridor toward the palace's north wing.

One of my personal security guards tails along behind us—Stephen, not Karl. Which means he hasn't yet returned from the Dietrich family's estate in Gentian, a small village tucked away in a narrow valley about twenty miles from Kapria's capital city.

So I won't have Victoria's answer before this meeting starts. But if she had decided against the marriage, she'd have probably notified me before now. After all, she's had twelve years to change her mind. I haven't received a letter breaking it off, so I assume she's still willing to be my bride—and Kapria's queen.

And if she's had second thoughts or doubts, she knew where to find me. My offices take up the first level of the north wing, and are situated beneath my personal chambers. Unlike the remainder of the royal residence, my offices have been stripped of the palace's opulence. No priceless artwork, no ornate furniture. The sleek decor and cutting-edge tech wouldn't have been out of place on the executive floor of an international corporation. Which, in some ways, is exactly how Kapria functions. When solving the kingdom's problems, I don't look to past regimes for inspiration. Instead I often look to the most profitable organizations and the most progressive governments. So these offices serve only one purpose: as a base for me to conduct the business of ruling a kingdom.

Jeannette's waiting at the conference table when we arrive. Add forty years, a sharp tongue, and an even sharper brain, and Jeannette could be a female version of Geoffrey—except that I've seen her eat. Sometimes she settles for food, but usually she just devours the people who stand in her way. Officially, she's my social secretary, but in truth she oversees the equivalent of Kapria's marketing and public relations departments. Every social media post, every news release, and every function that I attend are vetted and approved by a dragon in heels.

But even the dragon defers to a king. When I walk through the doors, she abruptly ends a phone call and rises to her feet. "Your Majesty." She nods to me, then to Philippa. "Minister."

"Frederich is coming, too." Somehow even more slowly than Philippa and I did. I'm tempted to start without him but rein in my impatience. I'm including both cabinet members because I'd be a fool to plan a wedding without advising the Minister of Foreign Affairs and the Minister of the Treasury of my intentions. "Let's go through to the study."

I head for the open seating area in the center of the

large chamber. This meeting should be short and simple. I've been betrothed almost as long as I've been king. Now it's time to marry the girl. There's not much more to be said than that.

On the sofa opposite my chair, Philippa and Jeannette exchange pleasantries and pour tea. I'd rather ask Geoffrey to stomp on my balls than to pass the time in the same manner. And where the hell *is* Geoffrey, anyway? I snap up the computer tablet from the coffee table and skim the day's political briefings. All the news is the same as it was yesterday. The whole fucking world is a mess. But with the trade agreement signed, with the Vic-10 out there, maybe tomorrow will be a little better for some of the people living in it.

And a lot better for the people living in Kapria.

Another ten minutes that I'll never get back pass before Frederich finally arrives. Geoffrey rushes in behind him, carrying a stack of folders. His eyes widen in helpless apology when he sees my irritated glower. Scampering over, he sets the folders on the table in front of me.

"So very sorry, Your Majesty," he whispers while the ladies and Frederich exchange their greetings. "The minister asked me to collect these from his office."

Frederich could have sent his own damn assistant. But no matter. He's here now, so we can get this shit done.

I don't wait for them to settle in before I announce, "I intend to marry before the end of this year." Eight months should be long enough to plan and execute a wedding.

"Jeannette, you will coordinate with the bride and decide upon a suitable date. I will pay for the ceremony with my personal funds but you will need to consult with Philippa regarding the budget for any related state functions, and with Frederich regarding the names of foreign officials who should—or shouldn't—receive invitations."

A hushed moment passes while Jeannette, Frederich, and Philippa share an uneasy glance. Then Jeannette asks, "Do you intend for Victoria Dietrich to be that bride?"

"I do." When they share another look, I sit forward and frown. "Why? Did she already marry someone else?" Another thought strikes me. Surely I would have been informed if she were in an accident. Unless it happened recently. "She *is* still alive?"

I ask Jeannette since she's supposed to keep abreast of events in Victoria's life, but I don't wait for her response. I glance at Geoffrey and he's ready with an answer.

"She is alive and well, Your Majesty. Or at least she was twenty minutes ago, when Mr. Sauer left her home."

Now those shared glances hold a touch of alarm.

"You've already made arrangements with her?" Philippa asks in a troubled voice.

"I sent Karl to inform her that I want to marry soon." Unless…shit. Now Geoffrey's the one who is looking uneasy. "What did Karl say? Did she refuse?"

"No—"

Satisfaction floods through me. "Good."

"—but she didn't believe him, either."

My scowl sends him stumbling back a step.

But upon hearing that nothing has been settled yet, relief seems to fill the three people facing me. Jeannette says, "We understand that you made an agreement with Wilhelm Dietrich, but—"

"But nothing." I sit back. "I have a duty and an obligation to marry his daughter."

Looking pained but determined, Frederich shakes his head. "That obligation was to a man who has been dead ten years. As no official betrothal announcement was ever made, very few people outside of this chamber even know of the agreement. You can easily choose another bride. A woman who is more suitable for your purpose."

Few people know of the betrothal for damn good reason. Victoria's privacy would have been shattered if I had announced the betrothal twelve years ago—or even two years ago. She could never have lived an independent life unburdened by the demands of her future position. Instead, at merely sixteen years of age, she would have been thrust into the public eye and forced to play the role of future queen.

From the date of my birth, I had been prepared for a similar role. But when I became king at twenty, I was still overwhelmed by the weight of the crown. I didn't want Victoria to carry the same burden. Not that young.

And I don't give a fuck if the betrothal was never official. I made a promise to Wilhelm Dietrich. I gave my word that I would marry his daughter—and two years later, I gave my word to Victoria, as well. While her blue eyes were swimming with tears and we were standing over her father's grave, burying him next to her mother, who'd died in childbirth years before. So even the Almighty himself couldn't turn me away from this course.

But now I wonder how much of a fight this is going to be. "You don't think she's a suitable choice?"

"She's a *horrible* choice," Jeannette says bluntly.

"Particularly at this moment," Frederich adds. "This marriage could be an opportunity to strengthen ties with neighboring nations and allies. Look instead to the sisters or daughters of the powerful political players in Europe."

"Or the powerful financial players." Philippa delicately sets her teacup in its saucer. "Give them more reason to invest in Kapria."

Both would be solid options if I weren't already betrothed. So instead the options are just a waste of my time. "Her father was one of those financial players," I remind them.

"*Was.*" Philippa emphasizes the past tense. "Now that family has almost nothing. An estate, a minor title, a little money. They hardly have anything to offer Kapria now."

I stare at her in disbelief. "Dietrich's money still pays your expenses, provides the electricity you use, and paves the roads you drive on. And the Vic-10 will continue providing for us."

"Yes, but the Vic-10 already belongs to Kapria—and so does Dietrich's money," Frederich breaks in. "So the

THE KING'S HORRIBLE BRIDE

question becomes: What *more* can the Dietrich family offer the kingdom? That answer is…nothing. And we must look to the future."

I *am* looking to the future. To a queen and heirs. But I don't need to fucking explain myself.

Philippa adds with quiet exasperation, "And it's not as if you're in love with the girl, Maximilian. You hardly even know her."

"That's true. I don't know Victoria. But I'm promised to her." And I haven't even looked at another woman since ascending to the throne. I might not love her but I'm committed to her—and she has my full loyalty. Which my advisors and Jeannette don't seem to realize, because they sure as fuck keep talking as if *anything* they say might make a difference.

"Even a scandal would suit the kingdom better than she would, because Victoria's real sin is that she's boring," Jeannette says dourly. "Boring boring *boring*. When she's not being awkward, that is. If you search the internet for her name, the two most popular photos are these."

She flicks open one of the folders on the table in front of me—one of the folders that came from Frederich's office. But as soon as I glimpse the contents, I realize they must have originated in Jeannette's department. Jeannette keeps dossiers on every public figure that I might come into contact with and briefs me before I meet them. It's no surprise that they have a dossier on Victoria. I've ordered Jeannette's people to keep tabs on her, but since she's the daughter of Wilhelm Dietrich, Jeannette would have probably kept a file on her, anyway. No doubt the other folders contain profiles of women without a single embarrassing photograph to their name.

Yet the dossiers were in Frederich's office. So he must have looked through them, approving a selection of alternate brides. And the three of them must have been planning this ambush together.

But unless she's in prison for murder—or unless she's a fucking Nazi—Victoria *is* going to be Kapria's queen. I wouldn't go back on my word for any less of a reason. Hell, and if the person she murdered was a Nazi…I might still consider marrying her. She could be infertile and I'd still marry her, then either adopt an heir or rely on science to get her pregnant. She could screw her way through half of Europe, and I'd still marry her.

And maybe she has. After that windup about Victoria being a horrible choice, I'm expecting at least a sex tape in her dossier. Something that'll require delicate public relations handling.

Instead I see a photo of a blue ski-suit stretched tightly across a shapely ass sticking up out of a snow bank, with a pair of skis splayed in an upright X, as if she plowed headfirst into the snow. Philippa winces a little when I laugh out loud—partially in relief, partially in amusement.

"The world laughed, too," she says quietly.

So what if they laughed? It *is* absurd. But delightful. And when I marry her, that curvy little ass will belong to me—as will the rest of her.

I move on to the next picture and my laughter dies, replaced by a bolt of sheer lust. The photo captures the moment she stepped out of a limousine. Either the wind blew or she misjudged the angle, because the photographer had a direct view of white silk panties nestled between the sleek lengths of her inner thighs, and the camera's bright flash rendered the delicate fabric partially transparent. Faint shadows hint at the sweet treasure hidden beneath.

With my cock suddenly feeling heavy and my uniform trousers uncomfortably tight, I slide my gaze upward. She's wearing a short black dress covered in glittering sequins. A night out clubbing, maybe. Her head is turned in profile, as if she's talking to someone still seated behind her in the car. A wavy lock of long, dark hair conceals most of her face, and the curled tips brush the upper curve of her breast, her lightly tanned skin exposed by the dress's low neckline.

Desire roughens my voice as I ask, "When was this taken?"

Jeanette says quietly, "Last year."

Then I should have gotten married a year ago. But the subdued, almost reluctant nature of Jeannette's reply makes me glance up. Jeannette is *never* subdued.

When I glance up I find their gazes averted from mine. As if they're discomfited by the sight of my reaction to discovering how unsuitable Victoria is. Except that's not what I'm discovering. And they must have misread

my silence as dismay. But I'm not dismayed. I'm more
determined than ever to have her. These pictures might
have been meant as a deterrent but they're having the
opposite effect.

And I'm pleased to see them. Not just because I'm
discovering that I want her, but because this was what I
wanted *for* her. Ski trips, nights out with friends. Years
ago, I ordered Jeannette to inform me of any significant
events or accomplishments in Victoria's life, but the
only notification of achievement I've received was for
her graduation from Oxford six years ago. Since I didn't
receive any other news about her, I assumed she was doing
what these photos suggest—traveling through Europe,
attending parties at nightclubs. Her father gave away
most of their fortune and assets but their family still has
enough money—and her name has enough pull—that
she could live completely unburdened and gain entry
into any social circle.

I'm almost sorry to end this carefree era of her life.
Almost. My gaze returns to her face and settles on the
curve of her cheek, her soft red lips. Before the heavy
warmth of my arousal can deepen, I glance back up at
Jeannette. "*These* two photos make her a horrible choice?"

I see her struggle for patience. If I were anyone else,
she'd have snapped a caustic reply instead of explaining
evenly, "Upon the announcement of your engagement,
millions of people around the world will Google your
bride's name. These photos will be their first impression

of your queen—a bumbling, awkward woman with a plain face and unremarkable personality. And these are some of the *only* photos of her. She hasn't accomplished anything of note. There's nothing about her that will capture the public's imagination. And considering that her father was a brilliant man, most will expect his daughter to be as brilliant and as driven. So her rather common intelligence will disappoint the public and serve as a poor legacy to the Dietrich name."

A plain face? The only remaining photos in the dossier aren't from the web, but from Jeannette's internal publicity files, taken at events within Kapria. In one, she's posing with a student awarded with a scholarship from one of Dietrich's foundations. In another, she's handing out ribbons to the winners of a village horticultural show, which is exactly the sort of ceremonial activity that the sister of a local baron might do, and that she'll be required to do as queen—though on a larger scale.

And she's not plain. Thick dark hair falls in waves around her delicate features, and her wide smile emphasizes the subtle point of her chin. Everything about her is pretty and pleasing.

Except for her eyes. Those are stunning. Though the rest of her features faded from my memory after our one meeting during her father's funeral, I've never forgotten her eyes, or the tears that transformed them into a sapphire sea.

These photos don't capture the effect of her eyes, but

she's still not plain. Maybe she's not beautiful in the high-cheekboned, fashion model sense, but she's not going to be walking down a runway. She's going to be in my bed and at my side, and the way she looks is perfect for both roles.

I glance through the rest of the dossier—pausing when my fingers encounter heavy linen stationery. A note from Victoria…and addressed to me.

I'm damn sure I never received it. "When did she send this?"

Jeannette frowns slightly, as if trying to recall. "After you sent the flowers marking her graduation, I believe. It's nothing but a thank-you note."

Six years ago. Scowling, I unfold the letter, which begins with the standard formal greetings and expressing gratitude for the gift. Then,

As I am no longer occupied by my academic studies, I humbly request the honor of serving at Your Majesty's pleasure, whether within our fair kingdom or abroad.

Always yours,

Victoria

Always mine. And as I'm occupied by imagining the kind of service I might have requested of her *six fucking years ago*, Jeannette opens another folder.

"Adele von Schuster"—she shows me a photo of an elegant blond—"of the Viennese von Schusters, and whose father is likely to become the next chairman of the Bilderberg Group. Here she is cutting the ribbon to open Kapria's new fine art museum."

"A perfect choice," Frederich confirms with a nod.

"And this is Felicity Pfieffer"—a brunette who draws a murmur of approval from Philippa—"whose family founded the Bank of Europe. She recently donated a new wing to Kapria's university hospital, along with a generous grant toward their Alzheimers research program. And here is Elsa zu Danzig—"

I laugh. "The actress?" And the only film star born in Kapria. Worldwide, more people would recognize her face than would recognize mine.

Jeannette isn't laughing. "During her latest trip home, she visited the children's cancer wing, which brought international attention to our national health program. And in a recent interview, she indicated that she would like to settle in Kapria and retire from the film industry. A match between Your Majesty and Elsa would capture the world's attention, as Grace Kelly did—and as Prince Harry's fiancée did."

"Perhaps we would capture the world's notice," I begin dryly. "But what *I* notice is that Victoria is also in all of these photos. Here, here, here." Attending the same events as these other women.

"Yes, but she is always in the background, Your Majesty. Even these other pictures"—Jeannette points to the snow bank—"she was only photographed because she was at the same ski resort as Lara Muller. This other one was taken during Chloe Schmidt's bachelorette party. She is not the one who stands out, except for the wrong reasons. Should Kapria's queen always be in the background?"

"Victoria will not be in the background when she is queen." And I have wasted enough time. Standing, I tell them, "My mind is settled. Victoria *will* be my bride."

Jeannette exhales a resigned sigh. "Shall I contact her, then, and persuade her that the king intends to marry? Since Karl apparently couldn't do it."

"I'll see it done." Irritation makes my voice harsh. But I won't risk Jeannette saying something that sends Victoria running. "And from this point forward, I won't tolerate a single word spoken against her."

"We would not need to. The world will shout what we have just said," Philippa proclaims, then appeases me with, "We will support Your Majesty's decisions, of course. Even those we disagree with."

"As is Your Majesty's right," Frederich says grimly. "We are only advisors. And you will do as you always do."

"And I will spin whatever occurs into gold." Jeannette purses her lips. "As I always do."

As if I'm ushering my kingdom into an international crisis instead of thinking of Kapria's future, as I have every single fucking moment since I was born.

I'm livid as I leave my offices. It must show. Geoffrey trots along at my side but doesn't risk saying a single word.

Karl doesn't have the same sense of self-preservation. He shows up beside me—apparently out of nowhere, as he often does. That ability is why he's the head of my personal security. That, and because I consider him a friend. He's also one of the few people who doesn't defer to my rank. Not in private, anyway. He does his job and follows orders, but if I ask him to tell me whether something is shit, he'll not only tell me the truth, but describe exactly how bad it smells.

But this time the stink is coming from inside the house. "What the fuck happened? Why didn't Victoria believe you?"

He scowls. "She thought her sister was playing a practical joke on her."

"And you couldn't convince her?"

"No." He hesitates before adding, "I didn't try hard. I had a feeling it would upset her more than she already was."

Now I'm scowling, too. "You upset her?"

"Or announcing that you wanted to marry her did." He shrugs. "Perhaps I wasn't the best person to send."

Maybe not. But it was done for good reason. As my head of security, Karl can not only judge what needs to be done for Victoria and her family to keep them safe, but he also moves like a ghost when he wants to. If I'd sent Jeannette or Geoffrey to alert Victoria of my intentions, the press would have pounced. But Karl can disappear from public sight when he wants to—and even when he doesn't, he's not memorable. He cultivates a bland, average appearance for that very reason.

Now he adds unhelpfully, "She said she's available next year."

Christ. I look to Geoffrey. "You have her schedule?"

"Of course." He must have familiarized himself with it, because he doesn't even consult his calendar before adding, "Tomorrow she's taking the early train into St. Moritz to attend the Women of the Future conference, and returning late in the afternoon. And she'll be at the palace tomorrow evening for the reception dinner to celebrate the Vic-10's worldwide release. Wilhelm Dietrich's family was invited, of course. Jeannette seated them at Philippa's table."

Probably to keep me from speaking with her. "Put her at my table."

Geoffrey pales. "Your Majesty, the seating arrangements required months of delicate planning and..." His voice trails off when he gets a look at my face. Squaring his narrow shoulders, he declares bravely, "I will go and battle the dragon."

"Good man."

As he runs off, Karl asks, "Trouble from the old guard?"

My advisors. Who aren't all *old* but admittedly have more decades under their belt than I do. Their experience makes them valuable to me, as is our shared hatred for everything my father stood for. But even when they look toward the future, they are also deeply rooted in the past. "Victoria was photographed with her panties showing. Google it. Or don't." I can't stop the world from looking, but I can stop Karl. "Just take my word for it."

He shrugs. "This day and age, the only remarkable

thing is that she was wearing any panties at all."

True. And I can't stop imagining ripping those panties off. Of tasting her. Of taking her. The world might see a bit of white silk but the rest is *mine*.

But before I can lay any claim to her, I need to make certain she's protected. "What's the situation with her security?"

Karl rubs his forehead. I remember him making that same gesture once while we were pinned down by insurgents and he was trying to figure out how to get us out alive. "It'll be a challenge. There's no wall around the estate. The house has multiple unsecured points of entry. And her sister left me alone with her in the garden without even verifying my identity."

Jesus. "You have until tomorrow evening to arrange a team." After that, everyone will know who Victoria belongs to. "The family will be out of the house attending the reception. Install what you need to then."

"I will. And I have a team on her now," Karl says, then adds, "A discreet team. She won't know they're there until everything is in place."

Good. I reach the White Chamber, where an interviewer waits to ask me about my kingdom and how the Vic-10 will revolutionize the world. To ask me how every step I've taken has been building to the moment I signed the trade agreement. To ask me about everything I've worked for—and am *still* working for. This interview is just another way to lift up Kapria, which has been my sole purpose in life.

But all I can think about is Victoria's ass sticking up out of the snowbank, and picture myself gripping her hips and pushing into her hot pussy from behind. All I can see is her sleek thighs and white panties…and imagine how fucking good it'll feel when those legs are wrapped around my waist, squeezing me tight as she comes screaming my name.

Maybe she *is* a horrible choice. Already I can't even focus on what needs to be done.

But I don't fucking care. I want her.

And I *will* have her.

Victoria

Before heading down the stairs, I check the mirror a final time. No makeup smudges. No hairs out of place. No reason to be so anxious.

But I am. A sick knot has taken up residence in my belly and my heart feels as if it's been replaced by a manic hummingbird. Because I've come to a decision.

If Maximilian doesn't at least acknowledge me tonight, then tomorrow morning I'm breaking the betrothal.

Which shouldn't make me so nervous. What would change in my life? Nothing, except that I wouldn't be living in fruitless expectation of a future that will never happen. My life is a fulfilling one. I love my work and my friends. And by abandoning the dream of marrying Maximilian, I could build another future. One that would be just as satisfying.

One that wouldn't keep me waiting.

Nothing would change. Yet at the same time, *everything* would change. That's probably why I'm so nervous. And why I'm hurting so much. Because even recognizing how moving forward is best for me, letting go of that old dream is like ripping away a part of myself…and that part contains a large portion of my heart.

Not that I've completely given up yet. I carefully make my way down the stairs, lifting the skirt so that I don't trip on the hem of my gown. I might not be a natural beauty, but I know how to make the best of what I've got—and protecting my image doesn't mean that *sexy* has to be a bad word. The violet silk deepens the blue of my eyes and accentuates my every curve without exposing too much. But there's still a tease, the slit in my skirt showing just a hint of upper thigh when I walk.

If Maximilian doesn't notice me tonight, then he doesn't *deserve* to have me, I tell myself firmly.

But I'm still terrified he won't.

On leave for the weekend—courtesy of a special dispensation from the palace so he can attend this event— James is waiting for me in the foyer. A grin spreads across his handsome face when he sees me. "Looking good, sis."

I am. But I'm struggling to contain the emotion filling my chest. Not my anxiety this time, but an upwelling of pride. Because he's wearing the uniform for the Kaprian militia.

My heart full, I tell him, "*You* look amazing."

"As good as you did? I remember that you put so much starch in your uniform that your trousers cracked every time you took a step."

I won't let him distract me with his teasing. "I can't believe how much you've grown."

"Aww," he says, then moves in and tries to disprove his maturity. "Give me a big squishy hug."

I back away, laughing. "Nope," I tell him. "I look my absolute best right now, and I intend to arrive at the palace still looking that way."

"The car is here!" Liz sings out as she comes racing down the stairs with her heels in hand and the skirt of her pink sequined gown lifted high.

"Car?" James heads for the door.

"The palace informed me that they'd send a car for us." Which would be an unusual courtesy for a mere baron and his sisters, but being Wilhelm Dietrich's children puts us higher up the list for this particular reception. Without the Vic-10, none of this would have happened.

We wait as Liz finishes putting on her shoes. *My* shoes, of course. I let her borrow them despite the prank she pulled yesterday—a prank that she immediately disavowed…then blamed on James.

Which might be true. Sometimes he's as bad as she is. And Karl Sauer might have been someone he met in the militia. A portion of Kapria's armed forces remain in the kingdom, but only as part of the search and rescue unit in the mountains, which is the post I had during my year of volunteer service. The remainder are sometimes deployed as part of U.N. peacekeeping missions, which is the unit James serves with now. He could have easily made an American friend who would be willing to play a prank on a sister.

Or I might be completely wrong.

Liz is the first outside. I hear her laugh, then a cheerful, "Good evening, Mr. Sauer! Are we carpooling to the palace?"

The blood drains from my head. Suddenly dizzy, I stumble to a stop on the first stair. Because the man who said he was part of Maximilian's staff is opening the rear door of a black car bearing the royal standard. I know who has to be inside that car. No one else in Kapria is allowed to fly those particular heraldic flags.

Rising out of the vehicle is an imposing figure I'd recognize anywhere. His dark brown gaze slides past Liz to settle on me.

The frantic hummingbird in my chest transforms into a soaring eagle, sending the blood rushing back to my head. With my gaze locked with Maximilian's, I'm vaguely aware of the twins pausing. Of Liz dropping a swift curtsy, and of the way James straightens, abandoning his boyish slouch. But I can't look away from Kapria's king, even when he finally breaks the hold his gaze has on me to focus on my brother.

"Lord Dietrich." Maximilian greets him in his deep, rumbling voice. "I humbly request the privilege of escorting Victoria to the palace in my vehicle. I have arranged for your car to follow."

As one person, the twins swing their eyes back to me. In shocked silence they stare for a beat. Then James recovers. "Of course, Your Majesty."

Immediately another figure—I dimly recognize Geoffrey Meier, the king's personal assistant—swoops in to greet James and Liz, and to escort them toward the second car.

Finally my feet begin working again, though I can't feel my legs. Or my face. But my heart, oh. There's *so* much feeling, and it thumps madly with each step I take toward my future. The king is dressed as formally as he was yesterday at the signing, but no longer in uniform. Instead his perfectly tailored tuxedo emphasizes the breadth and strength of his shoulders. And I'd forgotten how tall he was. When I met him before at my father's funeral, he seemed to overwhelm everything. But grief had been overwhelming, too. My heart had been filled with it then.

Now there's just Maximilian.

"I expected you to look lovely, Victoria." His voice is low, and as intimate as the dark gaze that skims my figure. "But you are absolutely ravishing."

I'm not a blusher. But I'm blushing now. My tongue tangles for the first time in years, but I manage an inane "Your Majesty looks very handsome, as well."

Strong fingers grip mine. "I am 'Maximilian' to you."

With firm lips, he presses a lingering kiss to my knuckles. My blush spreads to every inch of my skin. My entire body feels as if it's floating as his broad hand settles at the small of my back and guides me to the car. Separated from the front seat by a screen of tinted glass, the spacious interior holds two wide benches upholstered in buttery-soft leather. I slide into the forward-facing seat and, as he settles his big body across from me, I have to persuade myself that this isn't a dream. That he really is there. That I really am staring at Maximilian. Simply sitting in silence and holding his gaze.

But he seems content to do the same. Neither of us says anything as the car smoothly pulls away from the house. He appears at ease, with his long legs stretched out toward me, his feet on either side of mine, and one arm slung along the back of the seat. But no one who was truly at ease would look at me like Maximilian is. The intensity of his gaze says that while his body is at rest, his mind is busy—and that I'm his only focus.

Suddenly every second that I've spent preparing for this moment counts for nothing. I'm not usually shy or at a loss for words. A large part of the work that I've done for years is simply talking with people, making them feel noticed and paying attention to their interests—and there's no one in the world who I've studied more than Maximilian. But right now, *I* seem to be his only interest. I wasn't prepared for that.

THE KING'S HORRIBLE BRIDE

And nothing in my life has prepared me for the way my body is reacting to his presence. Not a single erotic fantasy or the touch of my own hands drew a response as quickly as sharing this confined space does. Every emotion that heated into a blush on the surface of my skin has burned its way deep inside—but I don't think it shows. I pray it doesn't show. Because I'm sitting primly across from Kapria's king with my pussy hot and wet, and with my nipples hard and aching.

On a shuddering breath, I clench my thighs tighter and subtly shift in my seat. The small movement seems to break the chain connecting my gaze to Maximilian's. His focus shifts downward, to my hips or my legs. I draw another trembling breath, looking past his wide shoulders to the darkened privacy window that separates us from the driver and another man.

No. Not just any man. Karl Sauer.

I can't stop my laugh. When Maximilian's gaze raises to mine again, his eyebrows arched in silent query, I tell him, "I thought Mr. Sauer was playing a joke on me. But he truly is in Your Majesty's employ."

His response steals my breath. It's not the smile that I saw during the public broadcast yesterday, which was unusual in itself, but a wide grin that seems just on the edge of a laugh. All the times I've imagined those lips, they've rarely been smiling; instead I've often pictured myself kissing the firm, determined line of his mouth until it softens. But from this day forward, I'll imagine kissing that grin.

I imagine it now as Maximilian replies, "Karl's in charge of my security—and he's a friend who can be discreet when necessary. But I suppose it is easier to believe it was a joke than to believe that a royal jackass like me could have a friend."

Delight ripples through me. Despite all that I knew about him, I didn't know he would make fun of himself, and it allows me to feel comfortable enough to tease in return, "But only an American, so it is not much of a recommendation of Your Majesty's character." But remembering how I'd thought that James might have known Sauer, I realize when Maximilian must have developed that friendship. "Was the acquaintance made during Your Majesty's service in the militia?"

Which Maximilian had been doing when King Leopold died, and he'd left the militia to take the crown. Like James, he'd been in an international unit involved in U.N. peacekeeping missions, which would have brought him into contact with troops from other countries.

"I did." Slowly the laughter fades from his eyes. "If you thought it was a joke, does that mean you believed I wouldn't keep my promise?"

"No." Truthfully, no. Despite losing hope as the years passed, my faith in his honor didn't waver. But a kingdom is not ruled by honor alone—and neither is a heart. "Not if you could help it. But life is not always in our control."

"Perhaps it is not." His voice deepens. My heart skips

wildly as he sits forward, reaching into his jacket pocket and withdrawing a small velvet box. "But I hope you will wear this in the knowledge that I will *always* keep my promises to you, Victoria—and that if it is my control, we will share a long and successful marriage."

Now I know this isn't a dream. In a dream, I would be able to clearly see the ring he shows me instead of viewing the glittering diamond through a sheen of tears. In a dream, I would reply in a strong voice, instead of a wavering and thin, "I promise to do the same."

Gripping my hand, he slides the diamond onto my finger, then gently pulls me closer. My heartbeat thunders in my ears as I look up at him. Softly his lips touch mine, then more firmly. A kiss to seal our promises to each other.

My first kiss.

My heart's a soaring, tumbling mess as he sits back to gaze intently at me again. Valiantly I fight to keep the tears that fill my eyes from spilling over.

Still my voice is hoarse as I ask, "Will we be making the official announcement tonight?"

"No. Tonight we will only celebrate the trade agreement and your father's invention." His mouth quirks into a smile. "Let those who notice your ring wonder about it. We'll tease them all a bit."

Everyone will notice a diamond this size. But even without the ring, the king showing up to an event with a woman at his side would catch attention. "And keep everyone talking about Kapria."

"That is the hope." He hesitates briefly, his smile fading and his eyes darkening. "They will be talking about *you*. Simply arriving at the palace with me will change everything for you. Tonight, a security team will escort you home—we'll provide additional staff for you there, as well. And you will need to ask your personal assistant to coordinate with my assistant and with my social secretary."

"I don't have a personal assistant."

"I will assign one to you, then. Or you may choose your own, but she will need to be vetted." His intense gaze searches mine. "You understand that from this day forward, your time will not be yours alone?"

I nod, studying his face. He's no longer at ease. Tension has returned to his expression, deepening the lines bracketing his firm mouth. I want to smooth them away again. "I understand perfectly."

Despite that reassurance, his voice has a rasping edge when he leans forward and takes my hands in his. "I am demanding a great deal of you, Victoria, by asking you to be my queen. Kapria will demand even more. Have you any doubts?"

"None." I have been serving Kapria for years. I know what the kingdom demands.

And he must know that I'm prepared for it. If a personal assistant is vetted, then no doubt a future queen is, too—promise or no promise. King Maximilian very likely has been told everything there is to know about me, and is aware of everything I've done for the past twenty-eight years.

And it all must have met with his approval. Because his response is to lift my hands to his lips, to kiss the back of each one. And those small caresses are not enough.

With my heart in my throat, I venture, "Your Majesty—"

"Maximilian."

"—may I do something that I have wished to do for a very long time?"

His voice deepens to a vow. "If it is in my power, I will grant any wish you have."

Instantly twelve years of longing bursts free and propels me across the space between our seats. Maximilian catches me. For a moment, the sheer joy of finally being in his arms overwhelms every other feeling. Then other sensations begin seeping through—the heavy muscle of the thigh that I'm straddling, the rock hardness of the chest that my hands are braced against, the firm mouth that's opening beneath my lips and the warm breath mingling with mine.

Then his big palm cups the back of my neck and draws me into a deeper kiss. A whimper of helpless pleasure escapes me as a hot lick across the seam of my lips coaxes them apart, and the breaking dam of pent-up longing becomes a torrent of sheer desire. I slick my tongue across his, seeking his heat and his flavor and finding pleasure that I didn't know could stab so hard and so deep.

Gripping his lapels, I pull myself as close to his body as I can, desperate to feel all of him against me. As I lick into his mouth again, Maximilian makes a rough sound in the back of his throat, a reverberating groan that seems to echo from my lips to my toes, vibrating across every nerve ending and bringing them to brilliant life. The tension in the hard thigh between mine is suddenly an unbearable tease, and I can't stop the slow rocking of my hips, rubbing my overheated core against that steely muscle.

With another rough groan, Maximilian wraps his arm around my waist and drags me even closer, until I'm centered over the iron length straining the front of his trousers. He grinds up between my thighs, the thick ridge of his erection stroking my clit through the thin barrier of my panties. My inner muscles clench in a spasm of ecstasy. I cry out into his mouth, rolling my hips to match the rhythm of his. My fingers clutch at his shoulders, trying to anchor myself against the frantic tide of pleasure, meeting every ravenous thrust of his tongue with a hungry lick.

Then abruptly he stops, throwing his head back against the seat, his teeth clenched in a tortured grimace. Doubt and worry assail my heart.

Was I too forward? Have I already made a terrible misstep?

Hands braced against his heaving chest, I look down at his face. An aroused flush deepens the color of his tan, except where tension has whitened the taut skin of his jaw. His arm still clutches me tightly against his thick erection.

This isn't a rejection, I realize. It's his desperate attempt to regain control.

"Forgive me, Victoria," he rasps. "I did not mean to take that so far."

I don't point out that I was the one who started it—or that I wouldn't mind finishing it. My ragged breaths pass through lips that feel swollen and hot, and the inner walls of my pussy are clenching hard enough to ache, my clit throbbing to the same beat as my pounding heart. I'm wound so tight that I could probably orgasm just by rubbing my clit the length of his cock a few more times.

But I'm also stunned. I knew that I wanted him. I just didn't expect this to be so…explosive. I don't lose control. I simply *don't*. But the fact is, I only meant to kiss him and ended up humping his leg like a dog.

Not that he seems to mind. When he looks up at me, there's only amusement and pleasure and frustration in his eyes.

"We should have taken the scenic route," he says gruffly.

Because we're already at the edge of Kapria's capital city. We will arrive in the palace within minutes—not enough time to follow through on this eruption of need, and just enough time to recover from it.

"I have no complaints regarding my view during this drive," I tell him. "I thought it quite handsome."

When he flashes that grin in response, I give in to temptation and swiftly kiss his smiling mouth.

I draw back before losing myself again, then begin disentangling my skirt from around my legs and his. His big hand remains curved around my hip, and he seems reluctant to let me go farther away than arm's length, but finally releases me.

I sit across from him again, feeling utterly pleased, and content to end this journey as I began—by simply looking at my king. But 'simply looking' tells me that we need to do more.

I open my clutch purse and withdraw a pre-moistened tissue. I hold it out to him, and when he gives me a puzzled glance, I gesture to my lips—which I'm sure are smeared as red as his are. "We want to tease the press when we arrive together, not scandalize them."

"Given a few more minutes, I'd have scandalized the fuck out of them," he replies and takes the tissue. "Unless I can clean my cum from between your thighs as easily as we can wipe away lipstick."

Now *I'm* the one who's a little scandalized, though determined not to show it. "I wouldn't know," I tell him blithely as I flip open my compact mirror and begin repairing my hair and makeup.

I assume by his silence that he's also cleaning the lipstick from his mouth, but as the seconds tick by, the air in the car seems to thicken. I glance at Maximilian and find him staring at me with an expression that I can't interpret—except that it's hotter and more intense than anything I saw while we were kissing.

With a deep rumble in his voice, he echoes, "You wouldn't know…about a man's cum between your thighs?"

I'm blushing again. I don't know how he does that to me. "No. Of course not. We were betrothed." Then I arch my brows and challenge, "Did you?"

The second that I ask, I wish I hadn't. Because I'm fairly certain that he hasn't been with anyone since taking the crown. At least, not that has ever been reported or even rumored. But maybe he was discreet. And a sick pain suddenly fills my chest at the thought of him sleeping with anyone else while I was waiting and waiting and waiting, and would have happily come to his bed—

"No." That fiery intensity in his gaze hasn't faded. "I haven't."

Giddy relief and an oddly possessive satisfaction roll through me. "My lipstick is still smearing Your Majesty's lips."

"Next time, it'll be your pussy juices all over my mouth." As my eyes fly wide in shock, those lips flatten with determination. "I won't wait until our wedding, Victoria. It's too damn far away."

"The wedding's not even scheduled yet," I point out faintly, still catching my breath—but also pleased. As much as I've learned from studying Maximilian, there's much more to discover….and his private face is apparently much different from his public face.

His mouth is also a lot dirtier. "Considering that I almost buried my cock in your cunt within a half hour of seeing you, at this point *any* wedding date will be too long to wait."

"That's true enough," I agree dryly, thinking of how long I've already waited—then laugh, suddenly recalling what I intended to do if I had to wait even *one* more day.

Eyes narrowing, he commands, "Share that joke."

I shake my head, not a denial but to warn him that it will only be funny to me. "Today I drafted a letter that released you from your promise to marry me. I intended to send it tomorrow morning."

I knew it wouldn't be as amusing to him, but I don't expect the reaction my confession provokes. He's suddenly utterly still, his body filled with the silent tension of a predator on the prowl.

"You were going to break it off?" His voice is dangerously quiet. "Why?"

I shrug helplessly, unable to articulate all of the reasons. But there's an obvious one. "It's been twelve years. And I believed you would keep your promise, but I also wondered if the delay indicated some...reluctance. Or if it meant that you were conflicted. Because you were promised to me but perhaps your emotions were engaged elsewhere. And if that were the case, I had no desire to trap you in a marriage you did not want."

"I want it," he says gruffly. "And my only mistress has been Kapria."

The kingdom. Which will always be his mistress. But she will also be mine, so in that we are equal.

I give him a slyly amused look. "And I will do everything I can to assist Your Majesty's efforts to keep that mistress well pleasured."

That fire lights his eyes again. "You only need to see to my pleasure. Are you finished with that?"

He glances at my compact. With a final glance in the mirror I nod, satisfied that my makeup and hair are perfect again—and no one will be familiar enough with my face to notice how swollen my lips are. I hold it out, thinking that he wants the mirror so that he can wipe away the lipstick still smearing his mouth, but instead he catches hold of my wrist and slowly draws me into his lap again.

"I will never wipe away your kisses, Victoria," he says and presses the tissue into my hand. "You must do it."

I don't know how this is even more intimate than the last time I was in his arms. But as I straddle his thighs and slowly clean the reddened stain from his mouth, the whole world vanishes. There's no Kapria, no photographers waiting, no reception ahead of us, and no years of longing behind me. There's just Maximilian, and his dark eyes that seem to memorize my every feature. There's just his strong hands lightly circling my waist. There's just the memory of his devastating kiss and the hope for a future that will be everything I dreamed.

Maybe even more than I dreamed. I didn't expect a fairy tale. But somehow, I've gotten one tonight.

"There," I say softly as I wipe away the last of the red stain. "We're ready."

"You might be ready, but I'm still in danger of scandalizing everyone." He emphasizes that claim by pulling me close enough to feel the thick erection still bulging behind the flat front of his trousers, and I burst into laughter.

"I cannot help Your Majesty with that," I say tartly, pulling away. "I suggest you button your jacket."

Because we've arrived. And now it's time to put to use everything I've worked toward and prepared for. I'll show Kapria's king that he won't have any reason to regret keeping his promise, and I won't make a single misstep. I've waited so long to fulfill this dream.

And it's time to make the dream a reality.

Maximilian

All the time I've been king—and the twenty years that preceded my taking the crown—never once have I resented the demands my kingdom has made of me.

Until now.

I just want another ten minutes alone with Victoria. Ten more minutes that I don't have to share with anyone else—or with Kapria. Because for the first time in a very long time, I am with a woman who doesn't seem to be looking at a king, but at a *man*.

And I hadn't realized how badly I've neglected that part of myself. Not just the sex. A king can jerk off his cock as well as anyone, and that's been sufficient for years.

But seeing the happiness shining from her stunning blue eyes as I met her at her home, then catching her as she leapt into my arms; the sensual longing I sense in her, and the way I want her so much in return... I haven't felt any of this before. And I want to wallow in it—and in Victoria's presence—for a little bit longer. I want to remain here in the car and kiss her again. Or simply talk to her. Because even yesterday, I was only thinking of sex. Of her sweet ass and the glimpse between her thighs. But now, after a half hour in her presence, I'm thinking of so much more. Every moment with her has been surprising, fascinating. I don't know what the fuck Jeannette was thinking, calling her boring.

She's bursting with life. First laughing at herself over the mistake with Sauer, then vowing to marry me and serve as Kapria's queen with emotion thickening in her voice. And although she's a virgin at twenty-eight, she's not repressed. Instead she burns with passion as hot as mine, her kisses bold and eager. And she doesn't simper in any way. Despite her insistence on calling me 'Your Majesty,' she doesn't show me any real deference. So few people speak to me in that honest, equal manner that she'd be precious to me even if I weren't marrying her.

And I'd sure as fuck like another half hour with her to make certain that she never thinks of breaking it off again.

One more day. One single fucking day. And I'd have lost her.

And I'd never have known how much I'd be losing.

Because if she'd broken it off yesterday, I'd have been disappointed but I'd have respected her wish. If I received a letter from her now, though, I'd do everything in my power to change her mind. I'll do everything in my power to see that she never considers it again.

As king, that power ought to be substantial. But Kapria demands my attention now. And every part of me that the kingdom doesn't lay claim to, Victoria has already captured. From this day forward, it seems I'll be a servant to them both.

I'll gladly be a servant to both. And the explosion of flashbulbs outside the car's tinted windows means that we can't put this off any longer.

Victoria flicks a glance at my lap, her blue eyes shining with amusement. I button my jacket as she suggested, then adjust the aching length of my dick so that the bulge won't be as visible. No chance of it deflating soon. My erection isn't likely to subside while she's anywhere within my sight.

As soon as the car door opens, shouted questions join the flashing lights. A fucking herd of paparazzi are outside. Kapria's a small kingdom and I usually don't garner this much attention, but the Vic-10 has changed that—and the photographers probably weren't expecting me to arrive at the palace by car. I live here; I don't need to come by vehicle. So the sharks smell blood in the water.

Victoria's blood.

But it's too late to tell the driver to take us around

to the private entrance. All I can do is attempt to shield her, taking her hand and making sure my body blocks any view they might have up her skirt as she exits the car.

But Victoria emerges as gracefully as the queen she will be, her face glowing. If these photographers are as incompetent as the ones who took the pictures in her dossier, they won't capture the subtle beauty of her features or the sheer magic of her eyes. I'll have to commission an artist to paint her portrait, instead.

The blinding flashbulbs double in speed and intensity the moment she stands at my side. She smiles up at me with that same teasing look as before, as if the paparazzi don't exist at all, though they're shouting for her name. I can't take my eyes off her as I slowly guide her down the red carpet with my hand at the small of her back. Then the paparazzi notice her engagement ring and it all becomes a deafening roar.

Laughing softly, Victoria looks up at me again—then beyond me. The slightly unfocused gaze that allows her to face the flashbulbs without being blinded by them becomes sharp and narrowed on one photographer.

Thin and dark haired, wearing a t-shirt and jeans and hauling camera cases that must weigh more than he does, the photographer doesn't miss a beat. "Tell us your name, darling!" he calls over.

"Please escort me closer to him, Your Majesty," she murmurs and I'm so bemused and curious that I do it without questioning.

Seemingly oblivious of the bulbs flashing in her face, she stops in front of the man—but she isn't looking at him. Instead admiration shines from her eyes as she studies his camera. "Is that a Hasselblad?"

"It is, doll." Laughing, he tilts it as if to give her better angle. "I'll let you touch it if you tell me your name."

Now she laughs, a bright and lovely sound that tightens every inch of my skin and hardens my dick even more. I fight the urge to escort her away from this cocky fucker, but the sheer pleasure on her face stops me.

She takes the camera and sighs in envy. "Who did you kill to get this?"

"Only the competition. I won Hasselblad's photo contest two years ago."

"You're a fine arts photographer?"

"That's me. But I still need to pay the bills."

"May I help you with that, then?" When he nods, she turns toward me with the camera in her hands and her face alight. "Might we have the honor of witnessing Your Majesty's magnificently imperious stare?"

I laugh and she clicks away.

"You want a camera like that?" I ask, already planning to tell Geoffrey to find one for her.

She smiles and shakes her head. "As much as I enjoy photography, I don't need one. My camera serves me perfectly well." She takes a few more snaps of me, then she turns toward the photographer again. "Sell those to a racy men's magazine if you can't find a tabloid that'll take them," she tells him, then adds, "I'm Victoria Dietrich."

"And will you tell us about that ring you're wearing, too?"

She only teasingly waggles her fingers at him as I escort her away again.

Over the cacophony we leave behind, one voice calls out, "Is this the woman your advisors called a horrible choice?"

What the fuck? That's *exactly* what Jeannette said. Tension grips the back of my neck but I don't turn or acknowledge that voice. My only glance back is to meet Karl's eyes. He heard it, too. Without words, I command him to find out who the hell opened their mouths. Someone talked about yesterday's meeting. Normally I wouldn't give a shit—I don't have any goddamn secrets—but when that leak disparages Victoria, it matters a hell of a lot more.

Karl will find out who talked. But it'll take time. So I'll trust that the leak will be buried in all the other news coming out of Kapria, including the forthcoming engagement announcement. Until then I've got no doubt what the purpose was. Yesterday three people told me that Victoria wasn't suitable. Now someone's trying to fuck with this marriage.

She's already wearing my ring. But somehow that's not enough anymore. Not after she was already so damn close to breaking it off.

But luckily Victoria doesn't seem to have heard the shouted question. Even if she had, she couldn't know that there was any truth to it, and her attention is focused ahead of us, not behind. To me she quietly says, "There is the Swedish ambassador, seeking you out before you enter the palace and everyone else can steal Your Majesty's time."

Fuck everyone else. Frustration boiling within me, I tug her to a halt and capture her attention by bringing her slender fingers to my lips, before turning to greet the Swedish ambassador and accepting his congratulations on the trade deal. I'm like a selfish little boy, resenting that he's interrupted my short time with Victoria—then a jealous little punk when he turns curious eyes in her direction.

"Victoria Dietrich." She smiles prettily at him and gracefully holds out her hand. "I'm pleased to meet you, Ambassador Nilsson."

"The pleasure is mine." He clasps her hand and holds it, his eyes twinkling. "You are Wilhelm's eldest daughter—and the one he named the Vic-10 reactor after?"

"I'm that Vic," she confirms. "And the number ten is because his invention went through ten iterations before it stopped exploding, so it not only bears my name but reflects my personality when I was a young girl." She pauses when the ambassador chuckles, then adds, "I overheard you offering His Majesty congratulations, but I understand that your own are in order—and not just for your country's part in the trade deal, but because your daughter Helen recently gave birth to a son."

The laughter in the old man's eyes is suddenly filmed over by a sheen of tears. "My first grandchild."

"You must be very proud. I imagine only the most incredible occasion could have pulled you away from her."

He nods. "A better future for them both."

Victoria smiles. "Then I'm pleased that my father's legacy is a part of that brighter future. But only a part. This would all have been impossible without His Majesty's tireless dedication."

I shake my head. "Many are responsible for it. I have done nothing alone."

"His Majesty is too modest," she says to Nilsson, before looking up at me and adding saucily, "You should accept all of the congratulations that are headed Your Majesty's way, for they are well deserved, and your shoulders are broad enough to bear them. As for me, I have monopolized Your Majesty's time long enough—I ought to move aside and allow others to bestow their humble gratitude."

Everything within me tightens and fights against her leaving my side. I know she will have to. But I am not ready to let go yet. I glance at the ambassador and the older man reads my unspoken request, stepping back to give me a final moment with Victoria.

There's so many damn things I want to do. Throw her over my shoulder and carry her off to bed. Kiss her until her knees give out. Instead I let my admiration fill my voice as I say, "That info on Nilsson's daughter wasn't included in Jeannette's dossier."

She grins. "I always do my homework." On her fingers she ticks off, "Political science, etiquette, public relations—"

I capture those fingers and bestow another lingering kiss. "You have prepared well. I could not have asked for a more perfect bride, Victoria Dietrich." My voice low and gruff, I tell her, "Once inside, we will not have much time to discuss anything. It'll be all small talk and bullshit. So I'll tell you now that waiting until October of next year is unacceptable."

A laughing smile lights her beautiful face. "Perhaps I can fit Your Majesty in earlier."

"We will marry by the end of next month." Because I won't wait until the end of the year. Her eyes widen, then her lashes fall to conceal the flare of heat as I softly add, "And we will take a full month for a honeymoon. You will be fitting me in night and day, Victoria."

Her breath shudders and she nods, her cheeks tinged pink. I press her fingers to my mouth, and the new explosion of flashes makes her engagement ring sparkle and gleam.

She's mine. And soon the entire world will know it.

Victoria

A few years ago, when I realized how badly my sleep was being disturbed by my habit of checking my phone every time I got a notification, I stopped taking any devices to bed. Nothing was so important that it couldn't wait until the next morning, so I began leaving my phone and laptop downstairs.

Today I regret not having a phone the instant my eyes open. Like a giddy teenager, I want to check my messages and revel in every single mention of my arrival at the palace with Maximilian. Instead I lift my hand and study the ring that proves I didn't dream it all. He really did ask me to marry him. And our time together was better than anything I'd ever imagined. The only disappointment was the expected one—that after entering the reception, we had no more moments alone.

Oh, but the moments we *did* have… I smile and languidly stretch, my body warming at the memory of his touch and his kiss.

Then I bounce out of bed and practically skip down the stairs.

In the kitchen, I'm startled to find James and Liz already awake—then realize that my brother's body is probably operating on militia time, and he'd never let Liz sleep in later than him. They're seated at the breakfast table, the early morning sun streaming in through the window and turning their auburn hair to a bright copper. Currently their heads are bent over a computer tablet, but the moment I walk into the twins' line of sight, Liz flips the device facedown on the table. They share a guilty, fleeting glance, then turn to me with too-bright smiles that say they're up to something.

Whatever they're planning, I don't care. I ignore them both and float over to the coffee machine.

After a long beat of silence, James clears his throat. "So, Vic…I don't have to report back to the base until this evening. Are you busy today?"

"I am." A pang of regret strikes me. If I'd known earlier that James would be home this weekend, I'd have kept my schedule free. "I have brunch with Sophia Bucklin in an hour. And then the job placement fair will take up most of the afternoon."

"I'll go with you, then."

Something's definitely up. I skeptically arch my brow in his direction. "To brunch with Sophia?"

"Yes."

"And you'll happily sit there and while we plan a fundraiser for the Kaprian Toy Poodle Society?" It's actually for the humane society, but I wonder how far he'll go.

A gleam of desperation shines through his eyes but he resolutely nods. "Yes. I like Sophia. She's a nice old lady."

No, she's not. And she'll try to hook him up with every one of her granddaughters…again. Sometimes I think Sophia is the reason that James volunteered for the militia in the first place. He was trying to escape her matchmaking attempts.

"And I'll stay home and spend a lazy day reading." Abruptly standing, Liz clutches the tablet to her chest. "I'm going to find a new book to download right now."

No. They've just gone too far. Liz can barely spend a minute with a book before searching for something else to do. She would never spend an entire day reading.

Suddenly dread weighs heavily in my gut. They aren't planning something. They're *hiding* something.

My narrowed gaze lands on the tablet. "What don't you want me to see?"

"Nothing!" Liz chirps. "I just need to catch up on my—"

"*Elizabeth.*" I use the same tone that I often had to use after our father died and the twins' parenting fell onto my shoulders. Then I gentle my voice and add, "We knew this would happen. This is what I was talking about last night."

I told them all about the betrothal on the ride home, and about the changes that would take place—changes that presented themselves almost immediately, when we were introduced to my security team.

But a security team is only the beginning, and we spoke about that, too. When I arrived at the reception with Maximilian, the gossip sheets must have begun scrambling for information about me. They wouldn't have had time to conduct interviews with my relatives and friends. So instead they'll desperately scour the internet for content.

I already know what they'll find. One silly photo taken during a ski trip, another picture that's mildly indecent, plenty of information about my father, and references to events that I've publicized and attended—which includes my connections to almost every social organization and charity in Kapria. If Maximilian had my background investigated as thoroughly as a future queen can expect hers to be, however, there's nothing they can dredge up that Maximilian wouldn't have already seen.

And I didn't make a single misstep last night, so there won't be any surprises this morning. In the future, I expect to see plenty of sensational headlines—most of them based on a kernel of truth and then blown out of proportion.

But that's not new to either Liz or James. As Wilhelm Dietrich's children, we've all ended up in European tabloids and on gossip sites—usually on slow news days, because even Liz at her wildest doesn't approach 'scandalous.' I'm not exposing them to a spotlight that wasn't already there and that they weren't already familiar with. That spotlight will simply be brighter for a while.

I join them at the breakfast table, set down my coffee, and hold out my hand for the tablet. "Let me see."

Looking uneasy, James tries to dissuade me. "Vic, you really don't—"

"I'll see it one way or another. You're only delaying the inevitable."

They share a glance. On a heavy sigh, Liz gives it over and plops back into her chair.

I wake the device and it opens to the article they had been reading. And yes, there are my greatest hits: my butt sticking up out of the snow, my exit from a limo all but flashing the good china. I scroll up to the headline, where they've posted a picture of Maximilian and me from last night. In my memory, I never took my gaze from him the entire time, but they caught us at a moment when I was looking off to the side as if distracted, which makes my bright smile appear patently fake—and Maximilian with his jaw clenched and eyes hard. As if he was pissed off but holding in his anger.

I don't remember him ever looking like that. But then, I was apparently looking in another direction. I think this might have been taken when I noticed the Swedish ambassador coming toward us, but I'm not certain.

It doesn't matter anyway. This is what the tabloids do: choose an image that fits the story they want to tell, regardless of the actual context. And their headline tells me exactly what that story will be.

A 'Horrible' Bride For King Max?

"That'll get some clicks," I say mildly and skim past the introduction which describes me arriving with Maximilian and sporting a giant diamond ring. I begin reading aloud when they finally get to the meat. "*King Maximilian's own cabinet of ministers has warned him away from the late billionaire's daughter. "She's a horrible choice," Maximilian's press secretary is reported as saying during a recent meeting to plan his upcoming wedding.*"

His press secretary? Surprised, I pause my reading to comment, "That's interesting."

"'Interesting?'" James echoes. "It's bullshit!"

Liz looks at me hopefully. "Do you think it's fake?"

"No. What's interesting is that I'm certain it's true," I say. "Even a rag like this can be sued. So usually they don't offer direct quotes—they'll just hint and suggest, using paraphrased statements from unnamed sources. But truth is an absolute defense and the people who run this site know how to cover their asses. They'll be able to back up the press secretary's quote."

"Then who is this press secretary asshole?"

"Jeannette von Hintze," I say automatically, silently reading on. I've never met her but I know *of* her. By all accounts, she rules her department with an iron fist. If this is a genuine leak and wasn't deliberately released to generate more publicity, heads are likely going to roll. I just wonder who will get to the source first: Maximilian or Jeannette.

"Well, I hate her. And you're not horrible," Liz declares loyally.

I smile. "No, I'm not."

But I can think of many political and financial reasons his advisors might want Maximilian to marry someone else. After all, Kapria's already gotten everything it could from my family—and as I skim farther down the page, that history is detailed as well, along with the suggestion that my father's donation made Maximilian feel obligated to marry me.

No, not just suggested. Said outright, too. "*A source close to the king reveals that Maximilian cited 'duty and obligation' as his reasons for choosing Wilhelm Dietrich's daughter.*"

But no mention of the betrothal. A strange detail to neglect, except that maybe it doesn't fit their narrative about me being a horrible choice, and would instead raise the question of why it took him twelve years to fulfill a promise. They have a ready-made answer to that, though. My gaze is drawn back up to Maximilian's quote.

Duty and obligation.

A sour knot twists in my stomach but I push it—and the tablet—away, shaking my head. "It's nothing," I say calmly, cupping my palms around my coffee mug to warm my cold hands. "They needed something to publish and they didn't have much. Soon they'll dig up more, have a new narrative to run with, and this will be forgotten."

"You're sure?" Liz looks eager to believe it.

"I'm sure." I haven't—and I won't—give the tabloids enough to keep that narrative going. I glance at James, who doesn't look convinced. "You should run upstairs and get ready."

He frowns. "Ready?"

"To have brunch with Sophia," I remind him innocently.

His eyes screw shut and he utters the groan of a dying man. Slowly he begins sliding down in his seat, as if trying to disappear beneath the table.

I glance at Liz, who's smirking at her twin's predicament. "Since you don't have to save me from the evil reporters and this article is all the reading you'll probably do today, why don't you save your brother by spending the day doing something together, instead?"

I don't have to ask them twice. They scarf down a quick breakfast and abandon the table before I even finish my first cup of coffee. In the quiet they leave behind, I open up the tablet again, close out the article and begin my morning ritual of reading the local news. But my mind won't focus and the knot in my stomach won't unwind. Instead I keep seeing those words flash behind my eyes.

Duty and obligation.

I can't figure out why they're leaving me so unsettled. It's nothing I didn't already know. Maximilian is fulfilling a promise he made to me and to my father—that's an obligation. As king, he needs to marry and produce an heir—that's his duty.

And I knew that love wouldn't be the basis of our marriage. Before yesterday, we had only met one time—on one of the worst days of my life. He hardly had an opportunity to fall in love.

That *I* fell in love with him…well, of course I did. I admired him even before our first meeting, and since then have learned as much about him as I could. Yet despite studying his character for years, still he surprised me last night. There's so much about his private self that I don't know and can't possibly love yet.

So I didn't expect love in this marriage. Unless I'm fooling myself. But rationally, I knew it wouldn't be a reason he finally married me. And last night, he only spoke of promises and keeping them.

But when he kissed me, I couldn't mistake his desire or the passion that burned between us. *That's* not duty or obligation.

So why won't this heavy lump of hurt and disappoint-ment vanish from my chest and let me breathe easily again?

But I think I know. I expected duty and obligation. I expected speculation from the gossip sites and to have mud tossed in my direction, and that the people around us—staff, family, friends—might say the wrong thing to the wrong person. I also knew that with one little slip, the media would make me its punching bag, or twist my words to strike at Maximilian. So I was careful.

Maximilian must not have taken the same care while speaking about me. I worked so damn hard not to do or say anything that might one day blow back on him, and I didn't give *anyone* much to hit me with.

And so what they managed to get came from Maximilian, instead.

Maximilian

"Anything yet?" I snap at Karl as my driver pulls up in front of the city's community center.

He shakes his head.

Goddamn it. That article had *quotes*—with names attached to them. That takes some fucking balls. But the number of people on my staff who could have leaked that shit is so small, they won't be able to hide for long.

I snarl "Find them" before taking the steps two at a time. I'm not expected at the community center and the location hasn't been fully secured, but I don't give a fuck. Victoria's here. And no doubt she's seen the headline that called her a horrible bride.

If she has, I'm not letting that stand in her mind a second more than it has to.

The dull roar of a crowd draws me to an open gymnasium. Inside are rows of tables and people lined up in front of them. There's probably an order to the chaos, but I don't take time to make sense of it all. Striding into the gym, I begin making my way through the crowd, searching for her. Geoffrey said she'd be here. So she'll be here.

Knowing that Victoria might have been hurt by that article pisses me off more than knowing that either someone on my staff or one of my advisors spoke to the press. Maybe my priorities are screwed.

They aren't. The second I spot her, I know they aren't. My priorities are exactly what they should be—and protecting this woman is as important as anything else I'll ever do.

Though she doesn't seem to need much protection at the moment. She's seated behind one of the tables, smiling and talking easily with the young woman sitting across from her, and entering information into a tablet with a stylus. Which is what's happening at all of the tables, I realize. Judging by the people lined up behind the young woman, I also realize that I'm going to have to wait my turn to speak with her.

I'm not accustomed to waiting for anything.

"Your Majesty!"

I glance over to see my Minister of Commerce rushing up. With all the bodies crowded in here the room is stifling, so he's discarded his suit jacket and rolled up his sleeves.

"Rashad." I greet him and then gesture to the crowd. "What is this?"

"A hiring fair. Kapria's businesses have too many open positions that need filling, and many of the refugees who have settled in the kingdom are skilled workers who need jobs. It's just a matter of matching them up."

Kapria's recent economic boom has served us well, but we have a small population—not enough to fill the new jobs that are being created. So many of the new laborers have been commuting from Switzerland. But this is better, especially if those skilled workers decide to stay in Kapria for the long term.

"A good solution," I tell him. "Well done."

"I wish I could claim credit. But it was Dietrich Industries that approached me with the idea." A wry smile pulls at his mouth. "No doubt at the suggestion of a minor shareholder."

"Victoria." Because aside from the one percent of stock that still belongs to the Dietrich family, *I* am the company's only shareholder.

He nods. "She also organized the first fair and has volunteered for each of them. This is the fourth in two years, and we've placed almost three thousand people. And it's not just Dietrich Industries hiring out of the pool of applicants now."

She organized this? Then why the fuck wasn't it mentioned in her dossier? I've gone over her file several times since that meeting—

That goddamn meeting, which is the reason why I'm here. Because someone opened their mouth. And I can't let myself get distracted.

"I intend to steal her away for a few minutes," I tell him. "And I need a private room to speak with her in."

"I'll see that Your Majesty gets one."

Rashad turns and raises his arm as if to flag someone down, but I don't wait for it all to be arranged. The young woman whose application Victoria had been taking is gathering her papers and finishing up. Raising a bottle of water to her full lips, Victoria glances over as I approach—and any hope I have that she hasn't seen the headline yet is destroyed by the taut expression that flickers across her face. As quickly as it appeared, it's gone again, but I know what I saw.

Seeing me upset her. *Hurt* her.

I can't fucking stand it. I bypass the line at her table. A protest rises behind me and is quickly hushed. That hush spreads a little farther with each step I take, until the loud cacophony of voices around us becomes a low din.

Either they're falling silent as they recognize me, or my perception is narrowing and discarding everything that isn't Victoria. She rises to her feet, a lovely vision with her chestnut hair coiled at her nape and exposing the elegant column of her neck. Perspiration curls the fine tendrils near her hairline. In deference to the heat, she's unfastened the top two buttons of her shirt. A black jacket that matches her loose trousers hangs on the back of her chair.

The coolness of her smile tears at my chest, because I can see the wariness that accompanies it. "Your Majesty."

"Victoria." I grasp her left hand and bring her slender fingers to my mouth, lightly brushing the backs of her knuckles with my lips. I graze my thumb over the diamond gracing her finger before releasing her hand. The mere sight of that ring sends relief rushing through me, easing the tension gripping my heart. Quietly I say, "So you didn't change your mind about marrying me, despite discovering that I've got rats in the palace?"

Her brows arch. "You feared I would break it off because of what some gossip rag reported?"

Yes. That was exactly what I feared. Because she'd been near to breaking it off only yesterday—and that was before she saw the headline.

But I only reply, "You shouldn't read them at all."

"Then how would I know what Your Majesty is up to?" Her beautiful eyes narrow. "In twelve years, sometimes the only news I had of my betrothed came from those rags."

That pointed barb hits its mark. Softly I tell her, "I am chastened."

"I doubt it," she replies dryly, but I see the warmth return to her eyes. "If I gave much credit to any of those publications, then I would believe in alien probes and chemtrail conspiracies, Your Majesty."

"Maximilian."

"Mak-si-mil-yen," she says, counting the syllables of my name on her fingers. "Maj-uh-stee. It's faster and easier."

"I will make my name worth the effort to say…or to scream," I promise in a low voice, and watch as an enchanting blush spreads across her cheeks. But aware of the audience surrounding us and of Rashad's approach, I can't do more than watch. "I've secured a room so that we can speak privately."

Her blush deepens, but there's no hesitation^{as} she hands over her tablet and chair to a volunteer waiting to replace her. "As Your Majesty commands."

As if my commands make a damn bit of difference to her. "Then I command you to use my name."

She shoots me a sly glance from beneath her long lashes. "You promised to make it worth the effort."

So I did. And when I gave her that ring, I vowed that I would always keep my promises to her.

We follow Rashad's directions, which take us out of the gym and into a short corridor. My guard Stephen stands post outside a door, which tells me that he's already secured the room beyond. I glance back at Karl as I escort Victoria in, silently conveying a warning that heads will roll if we're interrupted.

Inside, the air conditioning isn't losing its battle against the heat of the crowd, and Victoria makes a soft sound of pleasure as we enter the cool room. I'm aware of a conference table surrounded by chairs, but don't *see* anything except the woman with me.

She seems smaller today. Yesterday, she wore heels that raised the top of her head on level with my chin—and when she straddled me in the car, the height difference didn't matter at all. Now she barely reaches my shoulder, and when I pull her closer, she closes her eyes and rises up on her toes as if seeking a kiss, but doesn't get high enough to reach my mouth.

I could lift her up or bend my head, but I don't do either. Instead my gaze rests on her full lips…and this has changed, too. When I saw the pictures from her dossier, then saw Victoria standing in front of her home, then sitting across from me in the car—every time I looked at her lips, all I could think about was kissing them. But only one day later, I think about what might make them curve into a smile.

Right now I'd like to do both.

Still unkissed, she opens her sapphire eyes and meets my gaze. The blush has left her skin, replaced by a flush of arousal that she must know is burning just as hotly within me. I've got her pressed full-length against my front, my thick cock wedged against the softness of her belly. With her eyes full of need, she appears just as she did yesterday, right before launching herself into my arms. Because she'd wanted to kiss me for years.

Her restraint and patience must rival a saint's, because it's been less than twenty-four hours since I've had her against me and I'm ready to toss her atop the conference table, spread her sleek thighs, and devour her mouth while

I fuck my way into her hot, luscious cunt.

But I want that smile as much as I want a kiss or a fuck.

Slowly I trace the curve of her cheek with my fingertips. Her eyelids fall to half-mast and she turns her face toward my hand, as if seeking a firmer touch. I bend my head and she attempts to turn back and meet my lips, but I sink my fingers into the coil of hair at her nape, preventing the movement.

A quiver races through her muscles as I press my mouth to the hollow beneath the corner of her jaw. Her pulse thunders beneath my lips and, with my every breath, I fill myself with her soft floral scent.

"Your Majesty," she pleads in a voice thickened by desire, then moans as I drag my tongue up the side of her neck.

That sound coming from deep in her throat seems to stroke all the way up the length of my cock. Straining against the front of my trousers, my thick shaft isn't just erect but in fucking *agony*, needing more than the pressure I'm giving it by holding her close.

But if she can have patience than so can I. Reining in that raging need, I press a light kiss to her jaw. Her breath shuddering, she fights the grip of my hand in her hair, restlessly seeking my mouth with hers.

Holding her still, I tease the corner of her lips. "A kiss is also worth the effort."

That produces a slight smile, followed by a soft laugh. "Yes, it is… Your Majesty."

So it will be a battle then. Loosening the leash on

my arousal, I tilt her head back, exposing the vulnerable length of her throat. The two buttons she already unfastened reveal the delicate hollow at the base of her neck.

She goes utterly still as I unfasten the next button. And the next. I feel her gaze upon my face but I'm riveted by the skin I'm slowly uncovering—the ripe swell of her breasts, the shadow of her cleavage. She's breathing in ragged shudders that lift her full tits against the silky fabric of her shirt. Her taut nipples protrude through both the silk and the lace of the bra that I discover past the fourth button.

Just tracing the scalloped edge of that lace has my fingers shaking with need, the sensation of her soft skin against mine making my balls draw up tight and full. As if my cum's ready to explode out of me, though there shouldn't be anything left. I've fucked my fist so many times since I saw those pictures in her dossier that my palm, my bedsheets, and my shower drain should all be pregnant. The next time I come, I want my cock deep inside her, but more likely it'll be right here in my trousers while I'm stroking the soft curve of her breast. But I'm not going to stop at touching. Not this time. I'm too fucking hungry for that.

My cock's already dripping cum as I tug the lacy cup aside. I glance at her face to make sure Victoria's still with me, because aside from her shuddering breaths, she's been silent. But one look assures me that she's as far gone as I am, gazing back at me with desire glazing her sapphire eyes. When I reveal her breast, her rosy nipple looks as stiff as my cock. Maybe it aches just as much.

I know what my cock wants. And I know what's not enough. A touch is nothing but a delicious tease, because that stiffened flesh needs something hotter, wetter.

Her breast fills my palm. As I softly stroke that taut peak with the pad of my thumb, she trembles and bites her lip. To stop herself from pleading for more, maybe. Or to stop herself from giving in and saying my name.

In a gruff voice, I tell her, "Say it. And I'll use my mouth."

Her next shuddering breath deepens into a little laugh. "Please… Your Majesty."

Fuck. Because that sweet nipple will continue pouting up at me, begging for my mouth. And she's not going to give in.

I am.

With a growl, I lower my head—but the height difference that served me well when denying her a kiss is a problem now. She's too small. Or I'm too big. But there's an easy fix.

Letting go of her hair, I grip her ass in both hands and haul her up. She gives a little cry of surprise, then she grabs hold of my shoulders to steady herself, wrapping her legs around my waist. Her cry melts into a throaty moan as I latch onto that rosy bud, too hungry to go slow, to lick and tease. That's what I meant to do. To tease. To drive her so fucking wild that she'll be screaming my name. Instead it's me losing all control. Because she tastes so fucking sweet but her responses are even sweeter, a heady drug that I can't get enough of. With every pull of my mouth, her hips roll to the same rhythm, harder and harder, until she's grinding her pussy against my cock. Her back arches, her breasts lifting toward my mouth like an offering, like she wants me to devour her—and I do. I abandon her nipple, leaving it ruby red and glistening, seeking the other. Lace rips when I roughly free her breast from the confining bra. She cries out again, her fingers digging into my shoulders as I suckle her deep into my mouth. I blindly turn, searching for a table or a chair or I don't fucking care what, and finding a wall. I brace my shoulders and lean back, shifting the angle so she's riding the ridge of my cock, her curvy little ass filling my palms, her nipple hard against my tongue.

Then she gives a sobbing little moan, her fingers dive into my hair and she yanks my head up. For an instant, our gazes clash, the sapphire fire of her eyes burning with sheer need…and longing.

A husky "Maximilian" parts her lips in the moment before her mouth captures mine.

And I don't know what the fuck I was thinking, waiting to kiss her. Denying myself the heat of her mouth, and the soft helpless sound she makes in her throat when I suck on the tip of her tongue.

I should have been kissing her this entire time. Because my control continues to crumble with each stroke of my tongue past her lips, with each undulating roll of her hips. And if I don't end this now, I won't stop at all. I'll taste her mouth, then every inch of her skin, then her cunt—but only after I've fucked her against this wall.

Not our first time. She deserves better than a mindless rut.

With a tortured groan, I tear my mouth from hers and bury my face against the side of her neck. Hoarsely I command, "Tell me when and where I can have you."

She's shaking against me. Breathlessly she replies, "Any time and anywhere that Your Majesty wishes."

Your Majesty again? I bark out a laugh against her throat. "What about all that effort I put in?"

"You stopped."

"Stopping took even more effort than the rest." And I still haven't put her down. Letting her go might take more strength than I have. "What would you say to a man who wasn't a king?"

"I would tell him exactly the same thing." Tugging on my hair, she tips my head back until I meet her solemn gaze. "Any time, Maximilian. Anywhere. As long as it's with you."

"Then it'll be soon. But not against a wall. In a bed."

She nods.

"*My* bed."

That possessive demand makes her smile. "If that's what you want."

"What I *want* is to lick your pussy until you come all

over my tongue. I'd make you so damn wet, then feel your virgin cunt stretch around every inch of my cock." But even as her gaze lights with a new fire, I force myself to finally set her down. On a heavy breath, I tell her, "But what I *need* to do is apologize."

She doesn't ask why. Because she knows. That tight wariness returns to her expression, and the way she subtly withdraws to refasten her shirt is a spike through my chest.

"Forgive me, Victoria. When I called that meeting, I held it in my study, which is open to most of my office. I don't know how many of my staff came and went during that time, and I didn't stop to think how many people might overhear us discussing you." I hadn't thought there would be any discussion at all, but that's not an excuse. "I should have taken proper care to make certain it would remain private. I am sorry for that, and it won't happen again."

Her eyes soften. "Thank you."

I hadn't expected her to forgive me so easily. Because that's not the only apology that needs to be offered. "As for what Jeannette said—"

"That I'm a horrible choice?" Amusement lights her face. "And several of your advisors agree."

Remembering everything they said pisses me off all over again. Harshly I say, "Because their priorities regarding this marriage are not the same as mine."

My anger seems to deepen her amusement. "Did they give you other choices? Let me see if I can guess. Who's the right age and has something to offer Kapria?" Her eyes narrow as she ponders for a moment. "Felicity Pfieffer? Or maybe Adele von Schuster? She's very sweet, you know."

"I don't know." And don't care. I can't even remember the names given to me...although those do sound familiar.

But Victoria's having fun—and I can't resist that smile when she asks playfully, "So, who else? Tell me."

Shit. I do remember one. "Elsa zu Danzig."

"Elsa?" Her eyes widen, her tone teasing again. "She's definitely not a horrible choice."

I can't fucking play this anymore. "Neither are you."

"I know." She studies my face for a moment, then steps closer, reaching for my tie. I don't know which one of us loosened it, but I'm glad one of us did since it brings her within kissing distance again. But her eyes don't meet mine, remaining focused on the tie as she continues, "The article didn't mention that we were betrothed."

"I don't know why." But even as I make that claim, I'm pretty fucking sure that I *do* know why. It's because Victoria was the target. So they wanted to tear her down without touching me. "I suspect they didn't want the world to think that Kapria's king can be bought."

Dryly she responds, "I'm thankful they kept the betrothal secret, then. I don't want   the world to believe that the only way I can get a man is to buy one."

No one would believe that anyway, because the opposite is true. A man would sell the world to have her. Or sell a throne.

I frown as, for the first time in twelve years, it occurs to me that is exactly what Victoria might think. "It was your father who made the agreement. Do you feel as if you were sold to me?"

Her surprised gaze flies to mine. "No. I never thought that."

"Good."

She looks down again, eyes on her fingers as she tugs the end of the tie through the knot. "What about you? If *you* feel bought—"

"I don't," I cut her off before she can finish that thought. "And I got the better deal at both ends. I gave your father nothing but my word and received both a fortune and a queen. And my advisors could not have chosen better for me than your father did."

"Of course not. He was a genius, after all." And despite my attempt to stop her, she finishes her earlier thought anyway. "Still, if you have any doubts about whether I'm the queen you want, I would never make you keep your promise."

"You *are* the queen I want." And I'd like to strangle not just the source of the leak, but also Jeannette, Philippa, and Frederich for ever saying a word to make her doubt it. "My advisors will soon see you are the best choice, too. As will the press. But even if they don't, it will have nothing to do with what is between us."

"What *is* between us?" The stark emotion in the depths of her eyes is unfathomable when she glances up again.

"Duty and obligation?"

"Yes. Along with mutual respect, I hope. Dedication to Kapria. Attraction." My voice deepens, and I cup her face in my hands, tracing my thumb along the plush curve of her bottom lip. "I look forward most of all to the duty of producing an heir."

She goes utterly still. "Because even sex is a royal duty."

"A pleasurable duty," I remind her, because in that moment something within her withdrew again. But this time, I can't follow and apologize because I'm not certain what caused it. I'm only certain the smile that curves her mouth now isn't as deep or as true as the ones that came before. And although she doesn't pull away from me, the flat and faraway look in her eyes tells me that she's somewhere else, anyway.

Softly she says, "And it will be my duty and pleasure to help you serve Kapria. Because your advisors aren't wrong. At least, they aren't wrong in their reasoning. A royal wedding is lavish and expensive, but it will also boost interest in the kingdom in the short term—and in the longer term, offer another source of income. Especially from tourists. A royal wedding would receive free publicity on an international stage while the world's eyes are already turned our way, thanks to the reactor. So the last thing you want is to bore everyone. But with a bride who's beautiful, or flashy, or important, then the world's interest will only be heightened. Just like it was when Prince Harry decided to marry. That's why your advisors suggested that you marry Elsa."

I stare at her. She captured every reason clearly. "You might as well have attended that meeting, too. You just said everything my advisors did."

Now she gives me a dour look. "Your advisors are idiots. They think the prince's engagement in England captured the world's attention simply because she's beautiful? It's because they are clearly in love. And it helps that she's not the typical royal bride. She's divorced and was an actress."

"Just like Elsa?" My voice is low and dangerous, because if she suggests again that Elsa would be a good match—

"Elsa would be *nothing* like her. Because you don't love Elsa. Don't you see? A divorced actress *should* be a horrible choice, too. But in *that* case, her past and her occupation only makes it all more enchanting because love conquered all. It conquered tradition—and there are few things more powerful and more oppressive than tradition. So their love is like something out of a fairy tale. And *that* is what captures the public's imagination." A bitter little smile twists her lips. "But do you know what's boring? State marriages that are based on duty and obligation. If you want this wedding to keep the world's attention on Kapria, then you should pretend to be madly in love. Then all the awkward photos and horrible headlines that a tabloid can publish about me won't make a difference. Looking at me through that lens—the lens where you love me—the world won't see me as horrible, but adorable. And it will be part of the fairy tale, because your love conquered all, even over the wishes of your advisors and the insults from the media. So can you do that, Your Majesty? To serve Kapria, can you pretend to love me?"

"I don't think that would be a hardship," I murmur, still reeling from her speech. I also don't think that I'll have to pretend. Jeannette could not have been more mistaken about her. Victoria is every bit as brilliant as her father had been. Perhaps not as an inventor or a financier, but in her own incisive manner. "And I *should* have had you in that meeting."

Her voice seems thick as she says, "With one word, you could have had me there at any time." A sharp emotion glitters in her eyes before she averts her gaze. "We have not yet officially announced our engagement. If you prefer to find someone you can *truly* marry for love, I will release you from this obligation."

Fuck no. I catch her chin and force her to meet my eyes again. Harshly I say, "This is the second time today that you have offered to back out of our engagement. Are you hoping I will ask you to?"

Her breath trembles, and her reply is a strained whisper. "No."

"Then never speak of it again," I command roughly. "Some men might chase after a fanciful promise of love. I prefer what is standing right in front of me. And I *will* have you as my queen."

Because I can't bear to lose her now.

But when she closes her eyes and nods, then offers a stiff smile when she looks up at me again…it feels as if I've lost her, anyway.

Victoria

This should have been one of the happiest moments of my life. After letting the press speculate for a week, with Maximilian showing up at nearly every event I attended, today the royal palace officially announced the king's engagement. This afternoon, we stood together in the palace gardens and smiled adoringly at each other for the press. Now we're standing at the head of one of the ballrooms within the palace. Today isn't the engagement ball—that public event celebrating our upcoming nuptials is scheduled for next Sunday—but instead a more 'intimate' event for the army of staff and residents within the palace who probably won't enjoy a full night's sleep from now until the wedding.

While gazing down at me with an enraptured expression, Maximilian raises a toast to his future queen. The fiancée he's pretending to love.

I don't know why this hurts so much. This was my idea—to show the world a couple in love.

I didn't know he would do it so well. When the toast is over, he bends his head and gently touches his lips to mine—and for a moment, all the pain is gone, washed away by the pleasure of his touch. It happens every time he kisses me…which is often. As often as a man in love would. And not only chaste kisses, as now, but kisses that are hot and deep and so full of need that I forget sex is a part of duty and obligation. His every caress sweeps that knowledge away.

Until it's over, and I remember again.

Now he lifts his head and I can't stop myself from rising up on my toes, trying to hold onto the pleasure just a little longer. Trying to delay the pain.

As if sensing my reluctance, he kisses me again. So gently. So sweetly. As if he can't bear to let me go, either.

He's *so* very good at this. If I didn't know the truth, I could almost believe he loved me, too. He breaks the kiss but still doesn't let me go, instead wrapping his strong arm around my waist and pulling me in against his side.

"How are you holding up?" he asks me quietly, his gaze shining with concern as it searches my face. "This isn't too much?"

"Of course not," I murmur back.

"You've had barely a moment to rest this week."

True. I haven't yet cancelled any of my own appointments. Instead I added dress fittings and wedding consultations to my already full schedule.

My free moments have dwindled to nothing. I spend almost no time alone during the days and fall into bed exhausted each night. But it's better this way. I don't spend too much time in my head, thinking about Maximilian pretending to love me and wallowing in the hurt. If I did that, I would probably break down screaming.

Then the photographers could add that meltdown to my greatest hits.

"We can rest during the honeymoon," I tell him.

Predatory hunger sharpens his expression. "You think we'll be resting?"

I have to laugh. "No." And I look forward to it. A month of losing myself in his touch, and forgetting that it's all pretend.

"Tell your assistant to clear more time in your schedule so you can sleep," he commands softly, raising my fingers to his lips.

Then we're no longer alone, as Frederich Groener approaches us. The Minister of Foreign Affairs gives Maximilian and me a hearty grin. "My congratulations to you both."

"Thank you," I tell him with a smile. Perhaps he would rather see Adele von Schuster standing where I am now,

but his congratulations sound sincere—and after coming
into contact with some of Maximilian's staff and advisors
over the course of the past week, I suspect that to most
of them, the king's happiness trumps every other concern
regarding his bride.

After Frederich, we are besieged by more individuals
offering their congratulations, and the focus of the gathering
slowly shifts away from Maximilian and me, transforming
into a giant cocktail party. Lively conversations spring up
around tables of food and drink, small groups forming
and breaking apart. After receiving a line of well-wishers,
Maximilian and I separate to begin mingling—which is
both relief and pain.

I hate being apart from him. I hate knowing that he's
only pretending to love me. I hate knowing that it was
all at my suggestion.

I hate having everything that I ever wanted…and
complaining.

Determined to enjoy the party and to acquaint myself
with more of the palace staff, I refill my champagne and
turn towards a small group near the patio doors—and
find myself facing Jeannette von Hintze, Maximilian's
social secretary.

She stands about my height, with fierce red hair and
cat-eye glasses. Her sharp gaze cuts through the lenses
like green lasers.

"Victoria." A pleasant smile accompanies the greeting.
"How are you getting along with Ursula?"

My new assistant, who came from Jeannette's department. "Very well. Thank you for giving her up."

She waves that thanks away. "She's friends with Geoffrey, and he filled her head with harrowing tales of narrowly avoided scheduling disasters and heroic efficiency. So becoming the queen's personal assistant will be a dream come true. Did she tell you about the interview we've scheduled for next Sunday?"

"She did." With a writer from a major publication, and who has already conducted a series of interviews with Maximilian. After news of the engagement broke, he requested the opportunity to speak with us together. "I've opened up the morning to accommodate it."

Jeannette nods sharply, her gaze leaving mine to scour the lively room. "I must say that presenting this as a love match was a stroke of genius. I would have suggested it to His Majesty myself if I'd had any inkling that he could act."

Smiling, I point out, "He's always in the public eye. Doesn't that cultivate an ability to perform?"

It has for me. I can smile even while my heart feels torn in two.

"He's good at hiding what he feels. Not at faking what he doesn't." She glances back at me. "Karl thinks that I am the leak."

I don't manage to conceal my surprise—and then have to laugh. "I would, too. A scandal would have generated more press than Wilhelm Dietrich's staid daughter would."

At least until Maximilian began pretending to love her.

She tilts her head as if considering, but amusement lurks behind those lenses now. "That's true."

"But your job is to protect Maximilian's image," I continue. "Which also means protecting me now. No matter how horrible and boring you think I am."

Unfazed by my candor, she nods. Then surprises me again with, "I misjudged you. I've made inquiries, spoken to your friends."

"My friends…such as Felicity? Adele? Elsa? Or anyone else that I've brought into Kapria, so they can raise awareness for various causes that I discovered they're interested in?"

She acknowledges my response with a wry look. "I suspect you know this publicity game as well as I do."

Better, perhaps. Because I don't understand how she could *not* know what I've done. "Didn't you keep a file on me?"

"Of course. Though it was obviously not as comprehensive as it should have been."

How could that be true, if I was thoroughly vetted? Unless Maximilian didn't need a file. "Did he keep a close eye on me, then?"

Jeannette shakes her head. "His only focus was on Kapria. We were to update him if anything of importance occurred in your life. But much of what you did was under our radar. Probably because it wasn't your occupation. You simply seemed to have a wide social circle and a do-gooder reputation."

As I listen to her, I smile and smile and smile—though my cheeks feel numb. Though my fingers feel numb. I wish my heart was numb. But this pain is even deeper than the ache of watching him pretend. Because the only event of importance that he ever acknowledged was my graduation.

In twelve years, Maximilian only thought of me *once?* And only because Jeannette reminded him that I exist.

She lifts her chin, as if nodding to someone across the room. "You should go to him now. For two people in love, you've been apart too long."

So we have been. On deadened limbs, I make my way to his side. His loving smile when he sees me cuts so deep, I almost can't bear it.

I'm only glad we're not alone. With him is a familiar figure in uniform, who interrupts Maximilian when he begins to make the introductions.

"No need to tell me who this one is." Colonel Bist takes my hand. "Lovely to see you again, Victoria."

I smile wryly. "I wonder if that's true, Colonel."

He chuckles and looks to Maximilian. "Victoria served in my search and rescue unit… How many years ago was it?"

"Five," I remind him. "It was the winter that the unit received no rescue calls…except one." For a goat that got stuck in a crevasse—and after we rescued him, he remained at the lodge with us for the remainder of the winter, despite the colonel's repeated threats to throw him into a stew pot.

"That's right." His eyes twinkle. "The winter I went hungry."

Maximilian follows the exchange, then regards me with a puzzled frown. "You served in the militia?"

His question spears straight through my heart. *How could he not know that?*

And I fear that I can't completely conceal my hurt behind my smile this time. My lips feel tightly stretched over my teeth as I tell him, "I had just left the university, and wanted to be of service to Kapria. I inquired at the palace first but received no response. So I volunteered for a year."

The warmth of his gaze caresses my face. "You are full of surprises, Victoria."

But I'm not. I've never hidden *anything*. Everything I am, everything I've done, has always been out there in the open if anyone cared to look. But he didn't.

Yet I knew everything *he* had done. Because I'd been preparing for this role since I was sixteen. So I bare my teeth in a sharp smile and tell him, "You inspired me, Your Majesty. You fought for this kingdom's future and I wanted to do the same. So I wore the uniform. And after leaving the militia, I used my family's connections to bring in celebrities or aristocrats whose interests and donations might help lift Kapria up."

"So you were never in the background at all, but were the driving force." Admiration fills his eyes. "I truly could not have chosen a better queen."

Except he didn't choose me. My father did. And I can't bear this anymore—not knowing if that warmth and admiration is genuine, or if he's pretending even now.

I have to get away from him.

Wearing my smile, I turn to the colonel. "Please excuse me," I tell him, then bob a quick curtsy to Maximilian. "Your Majesty."

Then I walk away, as fast as I can—all the while pretending that my heart isn't bleeding in my chest.

Maximilian

When I gave her the ring, I shouldn't have said the wedding would be at the end of next month. I should have only given Victoria a week.

If it had been a week, then we'd have been married for three days already. I would have already spent three days in her arms, without a single event or obligation coming between us.

When she claimed her calendar wasn't clear until next October, she hadn't been completely joking. Add in my schedule, and I've barely had a moment alone with her—and those only in the car as we travel to and from events. Each night she returns home, and I return to the palace, because every move we make is captured by the fucking paparazzi, and Karl *still* hasn't discovered the leak. And although I'm desperate to have her in my arms, to have her writhing under me while I pump my cock deep inside her, I don't want to risk her being shamed by some bullshit tabloid for staying the night in my bed before we're married.

There'd be no shame in it. And it would be no one's goddamn business. But I don't want her hurt again. I just want to hold her close and protect her. Every day, however, Victoria seems to move farther away from me—emotionally, physically.

Except for when I'm kissing her. Then she melts against me. Until I stop. And then she runs away as quickly as possible.

Just like she did about ten minutes ago. We're attending yet another reception, this one at the botanical gardens to commemorate… Shit, I don't know what this event is for. This is one of Victoria's functions. I invited myself along because the gardens are in the village of Vesca, which is a forty-minute journey from the palace.

Forty minutes alone with Victoria on the way here was longer than we've ever had, and she came against my hand for the first time. I licked her pussy juices from my fingers for the first time. I'll have another forty minutes on the way back, and the only reason she'll still be a virgin at the end is because I promised her a bed.

But what I crave more than anything else is another

forty minutes of her softening against me, instead of stiff-ening and rushing away. As if she's trying to escape me.

I always know where she is, though. This time she went out into the gardens.

Slowly I make my way through the crowded reception hall and follow her. Outside, the night is clear and cool. Lush floral scents fill the air. Karl's waiting for me at the head of a garden path.

"How far?"

"Three hundred feet, cross over the bridge, then turn left at the hedgerow. Josef's watching her. He'll point the rest of the way."

Because her security team follows her everywhere she goes. "I don't want to be disturbed."

Karl nods. "We'll clear that section."

Good. I didn't expect to have an opportunity to be alone with her here, but I'll take it.

I find Josef, who directs me to a stone folly situated atop a grassy knoll. The structure resembles an ancient Greek temple, and an ache fills my heart when I spot Victoria standing against one of the columns, her arms wrapped around her waist, her shoulders slumped.

She always looks small. But right now she looks fragile.

Her shoulders straighten when the scrape of my shoe over a loose stone warns her of my approach—then her posture stiffens when she turns her head and sees me.

A blade slips through my chest, but I shunt aside the agony of her reaction. I strip off my tuxedo jacket to place around her bare shoulders. She looks stunning in her strapless gown, but I'd rather see her warm.

She murmurs a thank you, then tilts her head back. "Did you come out to look at the stars, too?"

"No. I came to kiss my beautiful fiancée."

I expect her to melt into my arms. Instead she closes her eyes, pain tightening her delicate features.

"Please don't pretend to love me when we're alone," she says in a raw whisper. "I can't stand it."

The blade slashes my heart again. Becoming my queen places an enormous burden on her. Am I adding more with my physical demands—and by needing her so damn much? Stiffly I ask, "Are your new duties too much of a burden? Or are you having difficulty pretending to care for me?"

A pained laugh escapes her. "*I* am not pretending."

That knocks the breath from my lungs. What does she mean by that? Does she love me?

I want that, I'm stunned to realize. I want her love more than anything in the entire fucking world.

"Except that's a lie," she suddenly confesses on a sigh, opening her eyes to stare blankly up at the sky. "I *am* acting. By pretending it doesn't hurt so much."

"What hurts you?" Instantly protective, I catch her hand and pull her closer. "I'll make it stop."

Another laugh escapes her, but this one is lighter, her voice slightly warmer—but also thick and full. "There is nothing Your Majesty can do to make it stop. Everything you are, everything you do…you are everything a woman could dream of. And more. You're such a good man."

Am I? I catch her chin and tip her face toward mine—and see what her voice told me that I'd find. "That's why your eyes have filled with tears? Because I'm a good man? Tell me what hurt you."

She doesn't, but tucks her head against my chest and remains quiet. The spike that seems lodged in my throat prevents me from asking more. So I wrap her slight form up in my arms and hold her against me.

Minutes pass in silence. Then she stirs within my arms and asks, "Jeannette said that your mother will be attending the wedding."

"Yes," I say gruffly. And it will be the first time I see her in almost twenty-five years.

"Is she being invited because you want her here? Or is it just for show?"

"I don't do anything for show. Why?"

She shrugs. "I didn't know what your relationship with her is like. The only thing I've ever heard about it is from the tabloids. And they all claim that you'll never forgive her for abandoning you when you were seven years old."

"She didn't abandon me. She ran away from my father." Who belittled her and gaslighted her and flaunted his mistresses in front of her—and in front of me.

"And left you behind with him."

"No. That is the part they all get wrong," I tell her softly. "She stayed as long as she could. She stayed for me.

Because she couldn't take me with her. My father would have never let me go. So she was trapped here. Until I was old enough to understand what she was doing, and told her to go."

"You told her to leave?" Her eyebrows drawn together in a frown, she looks up at me. "Then why haven't you spoken with her since?"

"We've spoken. She just hasn't visited Kapria. Too many traumatic memories remain here for her. Even for the wedding, I'm making arrangements for her and her family to stay in St. Moritz, because she'll come to the chapel for the ceremony, but she won't come to the palace."

"Oh." Suddenly she's searching my face, her sapphire gaze filled with concern. "And are memories of your father…are they traumatic for you, too?" she asks hesitantly.

I press a kiss to her forehead, smoothing away the worry lines there. "Not like they are for her. He pretended to be a decent man when they met. So she trusted and loved him and he betrayed her. With me, he never pretended to be anything but what he was. His abuse just taught me to hate him and everything he stood for—and inspired me to be everything he is not."

"So that's why you aren't a narrow-minded, cruel, selfish son of a tyrant? Instead you're just a little uptight."

"You think I'm uptight?" Maybe when I'm around others. But I barely have any self-control around Victoria.

"I said a *little* uptight," she teases softly. "What about 'rigid'? Do you like that better?"

"I'd say that 'rigid' describes me all the time." When she giggles, I cup her face in my hands. "And I came out here for a purpose."

Arousal flushes her cheeks. "What purpose?"

"I told you my purpose. But you thought I was pretending."

And I could never fake this. Not the hardness of my cock, not my desperate need to taste her, not the pleasure of every single kiss. I want to shout in triumph when her mouth softens beneath mine.

Whatever's hurting her, whatever's pushing her away from me…it all seems to vanish when I touch her, incinerated by the heat we generate.

I have no intention of letting it cool this time.

I kiss her, loving the sweetness of her mouth, loving the eagerness in her response. My tongue fucks past her lips until she's clinging to me, her arms looped around my neck, her hands fisted in my hair. But her mouth isn't all I want to taste.

Pressing her back against the column, I sink to my knees. She doesn't let me go, fingers in my hair following me down. Her kiss-swollen lips are softly parted, her gaze unfocused and slightly confused as she looks down at me.

Then her breath catches, her eyes sharpen, and uncertainty shakes through her voice. "Here…?"

"Here," I confirm on a growl. "You think that little bit of honey I got off my fingers was enough? I want your pussy dripping for me. Then I want to lick it all up."

Need darkens her eyes, even as her gaze sweeps the

empty gardens around us. "There might be photographers."

Leaning forward, I find the slit in her long skirt and begin trailing my hands up the sleek lengths of her thighs. "Karl's keeping them out."

Those legs start to tremble. "And if they have a tele-photo lens?"

"Then they'll be jealous as fuck when they realize I'm eating out this perfect little cunt. But they won't see a damn thing, except my head under your skirt." And they'll never know how fucking good she smells with her panties already soaked. Or how incredible she tastes, or know the sounds she'll make when I suck on her clit. But if she's having doubts, I won't do any of that. "Unless you want to wait."

"No." It's an immediate denial, and the naked hunger in her eyes is joined by a darker, deeper emotion. "I've waited long enough."

I have, too. So long that every cell in my body is starving for a taste. Her fingers tighten in my hair and her body quivers when I drag her panties down to her knees. The tuxedo jacket draped over her shoulders conceals just about everything that my kneeling body doesn't.

And everything that's revealed before me as I push her skirt higher... She's a goddess. A living, breathing goddess with the most exquisite cunt, and I'm a mere king humbly worshipping at her feet. Her plump labia already glisten with her juices, and her pink clit's swollen with arousal.

She whimpers softly in anticipation as I lean in. I

want to tease. To take my time. To kiss those silky inner thighs and work my way up.

But then she pants breathlessly, "Please, Maximilian. *Now.*"

Begging me. Though I'm the one on my knees. But there's nothing on earth I can deny her.

I go straight for those glistening pussy lips, that pouty little clit. Her flavor floods my tongue on the first lick and I groan, undone by her sweetness. She cries out and her body sags against the column, the new angle of her hips denying me another taste. My touch made impatient by hunger, I hoist her left thigh over my shoulder, opening her up and spreading her wide. With my hands gripping her ass to help hold her upright, I dive in again, my tongue thrusting into the well of her cunt before returning to her clit.

Her soft moans change to frantic little gasps, and her hips thrash against the firm hold of my hands. But there's no holding back when her body begins trembling. The pounding of my heart thunders through my head. I'm so worked up by the slick heaven of her cunt and by the juices running down my chin that my balls draw up tight and full. Molten drops of cum leak from my cockhead, my shaft milked by the agonizing need to shove past the tight entrance that I've only breached with my tongue. But there's no time to unzip, to fist my dick and stroke to completion. Even as she stiffens, then cries out my name with her back arching, what feels like a kingdom's worth of cum erupts from my cock. With a ragged groan, I ride out the orgasm and push her to another, my face buried between her thighs, her clit pulsing against my tongue.

When her body sags again, this time I carefully ease her down to the ground until she's kneeling in front of me, her skirt torn and her hair disheveled. Her lipstick is a smear across her mouth.

Utterly beautiful. In a gruff voice I tell her, "I ruined your hair."

"Fuck my hair," she replies tartly, then drags me in for an openmouthed kiss.

A kiss that I never want to end. Because she's soft now, with no stiffness in her posture and no pain lurking in her eyes. Every time she withdraws from me, it's after we stop touching. But soon—so goddamn soon—I'll have her in my bed. I'll touch her so deep and so thoroughly, she'll never be able to stop feeling me with her, inside her. And she won't run away again.

Until then, I'll continue touching her as often as I can, continue breaking down the wall she keeps putting between us. And tonight I'll eventually have to let her go.

Not yet, though. I sweep her up into my arms and begin carrying her along the garden path, heading for the car. I've got at least forty more minutes before we'll take her home for the night. Forty more minutes to have her all to myself.

Longer, if we take the scenic route.

Victoria

"The hair stylists will arrive at your house at four," Ursula tells me. "Makeup is coming at five. His Majesty's car will pick you up at half past six, and you should reach the ball by seven."

Unless we take the scenic route again. And if His Majesty is in that car, I'll probably spend the last ten minutes redoing my hair and makeup.

But I don't say so aloud, and if Ursula notices my amusement, she doesn't comment on it. Instead she surveys the table in front of me, as if making certain every fork and knife is in the proper place, though we aren't really here to eat. "Is there anything else you need?"

"Only the interviewer—and His Majesty," I tell her.

With Liz in tow, I arrived at the palace a half hour ago. Immediately we were escorted to this parlor, an extravagantly baroque chamber that overlooks the gardens, and served a light brunch. Shortly afterward, Andrew Bush arrived—almost as early as we were. But after Ursula informed us that Maximilian wouldn't be here until the scheduled time for our interview, Bush took the opportunity to ask Liz to accompany him on a walk through the palace's gallery.

And no doubt conduct an impromptu interview with Liz, as well, but my little sister is fairly savvy in these situations.

The door at the opposite end of the parlor opens. My heart leaps as Maximilian strides through, his expression austere, his big body imposing. The same King Maximilian that I'm so familiar with from years of watching and waiting.

Geoffrey trots alongside him. He flashes a helpless look toward my assistant just before Maximilian barks out her name. "Ursula!"

Immediately she snaps to attention, then glances at me hesitantly before answering him. "Yes…?"

"Solve a mystery for me," he demands.

She takes a huge gulp of air and squares her shoulders determinedly. "I will try, Your Majesty."

"How many years have you been friends with Geoffrey?"

"Four years."

"And have you *ever* seen him eat?"

Ursula blinks. Then blinks again, a puzzled frown creasing her brow as her gaze settles on the young man. "I…don't think so, Your Majesty."

"I knew it." With humor softening his eyes, Maximilian stops by my chair and stoops, softly kissing my mouth before adding, "Anyone that efficient has to be a robot."

Behind him, Geoffrey frowns at Ursula, his expression affronted. "But I *do* eat!"

Maximilian pulls out the chair next to mine, snags a plate of berries from the table in front of me, and holds it out to his beleaguered assistant.

"Prove it," he commands.

Oh no. Lurching forward, I snag the plate back from him. "Not this one."

Three pairs of eyes turn toward me—Maximilian with a bemused expression, and Ursula and Geoffrey staring at me in shock and horror.

Probably because I just stole something out of the king's hand. Smoothly I sit again and explain, "Forgive me for countermanding His Majesty's direct order, but my sister was here with me earlier and…I licked the berries."

Maximilian arches a brow. "You licked them?"

"I did," I say as matter-of-factly as I can, as if licking berries in a royal palace is an utterly reasonable thing to do. "Because my sister's an unrepentant berry thief, and licking them stops her from taking what's mine. But I'm certain Geoffrey wouldn't want to eat something that has already encountered my tongue."

"I wouldn't," he agrees hastily—then pauses and looks uncertain. Probably wondering if whether he should have claimed to enjoy his future queen's germs.

"I think we've established that Geoffrey doesn't eat anything at all. I, on the other hand…" Almost lazily, Maximilian sits back in his chair and regards me with a heavy-lidded gaze. "I also like to claim what's mine by licking it."

My body instantly catches fire as memories assail me, and I recall how thoroughly he claimed what was his—at the botanical garden, during the trip home, and several other car rides since.

With a smile tilting his lips, Maximilian doesn't look away from me, but his next words are directed at Ursula and Geoffrey. "Andrew Bush seems to be missing."

"He certainly is, Your Majesty," Geoffrey replies as he and my assistant head for the door. "We will go and find him immediately."

"Not too immediately," Maximilian warns them and a shiver of anticipation races over my skin. "Five minutes."

The moment the door closes, he captures my lips in a deep, blistering kiss. After rendering me breathless, he eases back, lingering over my mouth with gentle kisses before finally pulling away.

With a sigh, I let him go. "Only five minutes?"

A satisfied smile curves his mouth. "For now."

"For now?"

"I asked Ursula to clear your schedule today. You don't need to be anywhere until you have to get ready for the ball tonight. Geoffrey cleared mine as well." A slow fire builds behind his gaze. "And there are over a hundred beds in this palace. But we'll only need the bed in my chambers."

Understanding and desire twist inside me, forming a heavy liquid ache. "As soon as the interview is over?"

"Yes." His voice is low and gruff, his eyes hot with need. "Then as soon as I can get you in my bed, your cunt wet and your legs spread."

"It's wet now," I tell him wickedly. "Absolutely *drenched.*"

A groan rips from his chest and he lurches up out of his chair again, claiming my mouth in another hot kiss. This time he doesn't linger, but rips away and drops back into his seat, staring at me with a scorching promise in his gaze.

With a saucy little grin, I reach for one of the cherries on my plate. "You've met with this interviewer before?"

His answer is a slow nod. His dark eyes follow the cherry as I bring it to my mouth.

"Hmm." Breaking the cherry's skin with my teeth, I use the juice to paint a red stain on my lips. "And how did you answer the questions regarding our romantic history?"

"He didn't ask."

"He will now," I point out, and pop the rest of the cherry into my mouth.

His gaze lifts from my cherry-stained lips. "We haven't

mentioned the betrothal before. Should we?"

I shake my head, trying to ignore the deep pang that strikes my heart. "We're trying to persuade the world that this was a love match. An extended betrothal doesn't fit that narrative. No one will believe we had no contact for twelve years, then instantly fell in love."

He scowls. "Why?"

I shrug, because every answer hurts too much to say aloud.

"What narrative fits, then? What do people typically do? Do we make up a history of secret rendezvous?" His jaw tightens as if the very thought irritates him. "Dinner dates? Did we swipe right, and the rest is fate?"

"That's far too complicated. We'll stay as close to the truth as possible. Then there's less chance of being caught in a lie."

He gives a sharp nod, as if that's a more satisfying solution. "All right. The truth. Mostly."

Yes, mostly. Except for the part where he's pretending to love me.

My throat tightens. Watching me, he seems to sense the change in my emotions. His eyes narrow, and he slowly rises from his chair. Intending to kiss me again.

I'd rather have the pleasure than the pain. I lift my mouth to meet his, and he slowly kisses my upper lip, then my lower lip, then licks away the cherry stain.

Through the blissful haze, I'm aware of the parlor door opening, of Liz's and Ursula's voices—and the abrupt silence, as if they suddenly realized what Maximilian and I were doing. But he doesn't quickly draw away. Instead his dark gaze holds mine for an endless time.

When he finally retreats, it's with another kiss and a gruff, "An hour from now, I'll have your cherry juice all over my cock," spoken quietly against my ear.

I'm so dizzy with anticipation and need that I barely notice when Liz and our assistants leave again, and Andrew Bush takes his seat. With wire-rim glasses, a wiry build swimming in an oversized suit over a collared sport shirt, he resembles every mild-mannered journalist I've ever seen in movies or television. But after reading some of his work, I suspect that 'mild-mannered' fits him as well as a donkey's boot. His observations are sharp, but often infused with warmth and humanity. As if he's truly looking for stories to tell, not just lining up jugulars to cut. Of course, that doesn't mean his articles haven't sliced some of his subjects' throats open.

I pour the coffee as he begins by offering his congratulations on our engagement. Setting the cup in front of him, I sit back in my chair and say, "I see that you're married as well." I gesture to the gold band on his finger. "Do you have any advice to offer a pair of newlyweds?"

"Where do you want me to start?" He laughs, but his gaze turns serious a moment later. "Be true to yourself and recognize your needs—then make certain to communicate those needs."

Perhaps easier said than done. "Does communicating

come easily to someone like you—a man who writes for a living?"

"I wish. Whenever my husband and I get into an argument, I can't say a damn thing right. Then I'll write him a ten-page email and finally manage to explain myself." Abruptly he grins. "And Liz warned me that you always do your homework, and that you'll end up interviewing me instead of the other way around."

I smile innocently and sip my coffee. "What would you like to ask?"

"We'll start with a simple one. Where did you two meet?"

"The first time? When we were burying my father."

He grimaces. "I'm sorry. That wasn't a romantic meeting, then."

"No, it wasn't," I say softly, and stay as near to the truth as I can. "We didn't meet again until fairly recently."

"And you must have both played your renewed acquaintance close to your vests." To Maximilian, he says, "You didn't mention her at all during our recent series of interviews."

"You didn't ask," Maximilian replies dryly.

"But if you only recently met Victoria again, this relationship must have also developed recently—and quickly."

"You might say instantly." His dark gaze warms as he looks to me. "I saw her standing in front of her house. Thirty minutes later I knew that I'd never want anyone else."

"That quickly?" Andrew's brows rise.

Maximilian nods. "I know it sounds unbelievable. But

it's true."

Mostly true. And all pretend. My throat aching, I don't let myself imagine that it could be anything else.

"So what was different about her?"

"Different from the first time I met her?" Maximilian frowns. "She was ten years older. And wasn't crying."

Andrew shakes his head. "I meant— As the king of Kapria, you must have encountered many beautiful and accomplished women. Yet you've never been attached to any of them. Not publicly, at least."

"Not privately, either."

"So why was your reaction to Victoria so different?"

Because he was betrothed to me. Because he'd made a promise and he kept it. But he can't respond with that truth, or anything close to it. And I don't know what to make of what he does respond with.

"It was different because there *was* a reaction." He frowns at the interviewer. "Before meeting Victoria again, I was only a king. My only thoughts were of Kapria. When I met women, I didn't see them as potential lovers. I only saw what needed to be done to help my people."

The ache in my chest expands. I could have helped him. All those years, I *wanted* to help him. And I did what I could, though I would have loved to work beside him to do more.

But he was blind to that, too.

"So it sounds like the real change was your success with the Vic-10, and negotiating the trade agreement.

It allowed you to broaden your focus."

Maximilian nods. "And the burden of healing the damage from my father's reign was a lighter one, so I could imagine taking on other responsibilities. A queen, heirs. So when it was time to take a wife, I could look at women differently. But I didn't need to look past Victoria. She is more perfect for me than any other woman I could possibly imagine."

Because I worked so hard to be perfect for the role I saw myself in. But it is nothing like the role that Maximilian imagines me filling.

My heart feels sick and heavy in my chest, my throat raw when Andrew seems finally satisfied with that answer and turns to me again.

"So it's been a whirlwind for you, too?"

"No." It's a thick, quiet rasp, overfilled with emotion. And true. "I fell in love with His Majesty when I was sixteen years old—on the day of his coronation, when he stood and delivered that speech. That angry, wonderful, inspiring speech."

"I've seen it," Andrew says quietly.

Of course he has. He probably watched it in preparation for this assignment. But that's not how I saw it. Not as homework or research, but one of the most pivotal moments of my life.

"I watched it with my father. He hated having to flee Kapria when Leopold took the throne, and he always dreamed of going home—but to me, after hearing him speak of the kingdom for sixteen years, Kapria didn't even seem like a real place. More like a fairytale land ruled by a villainous king. So when we watched the coronation and the speech, I thought I would witness the rise of a spoiled brat prince who would only bring more pain to my father's heart." Tears blur my eyes and ache in my throat. "But Maximilian gave my father hope, instead. And watching all that fury, listening to him promise that he wouldn't rest until he'd secured a new future for the kingdom, I was so *inspired*…and determined to do the same."

This time Andrew doesn't respond. And I'm aware of Maximilian's utter silence, and the burning weight of his gaze upon me, but I don't look.

After a moment, I continue, "When I'm interviewed, people almost always ask whether I resent my father for giving so much to the Kaprian king, and barely leaving his family anything. But we Dietrichs are very good at giving everything away. I gave all that I am to Kapria and her king that day, too—and I didn't hold much back. Certainly not my heart."

Andrew fiddles with his papers, seems at a loss for words—but when finally he speaks, I can hear the thickening of his voice, as if affected by strong emotion. "And when you met him again? Did he live up to your father's hopes…and your own?"

I laugh at the absurdity of the question. "Have you seen what he has done for Kapria? He has far surpassed our hopes."

He glances at Maximilian, but I don't have the courage to do the same. "So have you been pining for him these twelve years?"

There's a lighter, teasing note in his voice, but I feel the seriousness of the question behind it all the same. "Of course not," I tell him, attempting the same light note. "He didn't inspire me to sit at home, waiting for him to come and sweep me into his arms. I got to work serving Kapria, instead."

"By all accounts, you've served the kingdom well." He smiles—then abruptly sits back, eyes flying wide.

Maximilian's suddenly in front of me, his eyes like burning coals amid the stark, granite beauty of his face. Then the world shifts and tilts as he hauls me out of the chair, sweeping me up to cradle my body against his chest.

Without a word to the interviewer, he strides for the door. Off balance despite the firm support of his arms, I can only witness in amazement as we abandon a stunned Andrew—then pass a surprised Geoffrey and Ursula. Whatever they see in Maximilian's expression sends them back a step, and instead of falling in behind us, they simply watch Maximilian continue carrying me down the corridor.

Suddenly I know where we are going. And the hot anticipation of finally being in his bed still smolders within me, but there's more, molten anger that roils just beneath my heart—and the pain that chokes my throat with a jagged lump of suppressed emotion.

Maximilian pushes through the doors to his private quarters. But instead of carrying me through to a bedchamber, suddenly he sets me down and crowds me back against a wall. His face is a pale mask of tension as he looms over me, bending his head—but not to kiss me. His eyes are a blazing fire as his gaze searches mine.

Hoarsely he asks, "Is it true? What you told him. Is it true?"

The painful lump in my throat grows. "What part?"

Still rigid with tension, he doesn't look away from my face, giving me nowhere to hide. "The part where you loved me since you were sixteen."

"Yes," I whisper—then the relief and joy that sweeps over his expression is like a pin piercing the balloon of all the painful emotions that have been swelling inside me these past few weeks. For the past twelve *years*. But instead of popping open in an explosion of anger, it leaks out in sudden, uncontrollable tears. "Even though I was *nothing* to you."

He freezes at the sight of my tears, voice filled with alarm. "Victoria?"

"All this time." My breath is suddenly hitching, and I fight against the sobs that struggle to burst free. "I was nothing to you. And I'm not a sixteen year old girl anymore. You were the world to me—but even after we were betrothed, I didn't expect to be your sun and your moon. Yet I should have been *something*! But in twelve years, you barely gave me a passing thought." And as the enormity of that truth crashes into me, the first sob rips from my throat. "And what kind of marriage will this be, when I've been nothing to you for so long? How many years until I'm nothing again? After I've popped out an heir and a spare?"

Face white, he shakes his head. "You aren't nothing to me, Victoria. You never were. You're everything."

"Am I?" I lift my gaze to his, not even trying to wipe away the tears sliding down my cheeks. "In those twelve years, how many times did you think of me? How many times did you wonder what I was doing, what I was thinking? Because it's obvious you never bothered to find out."

"I was supposed to be told—"

"No, Maximilian," I say softly. The enormous pain in my chest still grows, but a calm has suddenly joined it, soothing my shuddering breaths. As if I'd *needed* that eruption before I could move on. "You are a king. You set the tone and the direction of everything in your domain. So you told them one time to keep tabs on me. But after that? Years passed. And they weren't interested in knowing what I was doing because *you* never showed any interest. But if you'd asked about me even once a year, then they'd have paid closer attention."

His eyes close as if in pain. Because he knows that's true. And his voice is raw as he says, "I *did* think of you, Victoria. And when I heard nothing from Jeannette, I assumed you were doing all the carefree things that young women in your position do. I was happy for you."

"Happy for me...because you thought I was a social-ite?" I stare at him in disbelief. "I've never wanted that kind of life."

"I just didn't want you burdened with a queen's respon-sibilities when you were so young. Because I knew how heavy they were." He meets my gaze again. "But you shouldered those burdens anyway, serving Kapria all this time."

"That wasn't a burden to *me*." Renewed tears burn in my throat. "Why did you never ask me what I wanted?"

A bleak expression passes over his face. "I thought I was doing what was best."

"And you decided what was best without consulting me?" A painful laugh hitches my chest. "Of course you did. You're a king. You can make decisions for everyone without asking what they want. But even my father asked me before agreeing to our betrothal. He made sure it was my decision. He didn't just give me to you. He asked me if it was what I wanted. And it was." A sobbing breath shudders free. "Marrying you was everything I could possibly want."

"*Was?*" He's utterly still. "But it isn't now?"

"I don't know if it is anymore," I whisper brokenly.

A rough denial seems ripped from him and he pushes closer, catching my face in his big hands, his eyes tortured. "But you *love* me."

"I do." So much that it keeps breaking my heart open. "But that's not all that a marriage is. And I have spent twelve years imagining what being your queen would be like. I've worked so hard, so I could step into that role."

"I know how much you have done," he says gruffly. "I *know* that about you now."

"But the role I pictured for myself, and the role you have planned for me—they couldn't be any more different!" For a moment I can't continue, the pain closing my throat again. "I thought a queen would be a partner to help you share your burdens. But you see a wife as yet another responsibility, a new burden to bear now that Kapria is not so heavy on your shoulders. You aren't looking for a partner. You're looking for a bedmate and a breeder. And although I want to be with you, to have children with you…in a marriage, I want to be more than that."

"Then you'll be more than that. You *are* more than that," he adds fiercely. "And whatever you want your role as queen to be, that is what it will be."

"Truly?" I want to hope but I don't know if I can. "Because you seem to hate the thought of burdening me with *anything*. Why would I believe you would share them, and decide what's best for me again?"

"Because if it means you will be my queen, I will do anything. *Anything*," he vows through clenched teeth.

"For Kapria?" Of course he would.

"For *me*." A rough laugh breaks from him. "I want you for *me*, Victoria. But if I have to, I'll share you with my kingdom. Even if I resent every single goddamn second that Kapria takes you away from me."

"You resent what?" I shake my head, trying to understand. "What are you saying?"

"That you were right," he says softly now, brushing the tears from my cheeks with a sweep of his thumbs. "All these years that we were betrothed, I only thought of you as the woman who would give me my heirs. Because I was only thinking of you in the way a king thinks of his future queen. And that's all I was: a king. I wanted to be everything my father wasn't. He only thought of himself, and so I only let myself think of Kapria, of my duties and obligations. I was never selfish. I never looked at anything as *mine*. Until you. And suddenly I was more than a king. I was a man who wanted Victoria Dietrich more than I've wanted anything."

I stare at him through a sheen of tears, too overwhelmed by the emotions clogging my throat to speak.

Tenderly he lifts my left hand to his mouth, brushes his lips over the glittering diamond. "Do I want to keep you in my bed and pregnant? I'd love to. But only if I'm in that bed, too. I'd lock you away in a tower, but only if I was there with you. But since I have to be king, too…I'll share everything I am with you, just so that I can keep you beside me as much as I can." His voice hoarsens again, his gaze burning into mine. "So will you marry this selfish man and be the kind of queen you've always wanted to be?"

My tears spill over again. "I will."

"Wise choice," he murmurs against my mouth. "Because

if you'd said no, I'd have locked us together in a tower, anyway."

A laugh rolls through me, and I feel his smile against my own before he claims my lips. His tongue coaxes them apart with a possessive lick even as he sweeps me up into his arms again. Lost in his kiss and the blissful happiness racing through me, I don't see any of the rooms that we pass through. I don't feel anything but Maximilian until he eases me down onto a blue silk bedspread. Stepping back, he abruptly yanks my skirt down the length of my legs, letting it drop the floor.

"Next time, I'll do this part right," he says gruffly, grips the hem of my shirt and tugs it up over my head. "I'll slowly peel your clothes off"—my bra is next, the fastenings disregarded and the whole thing dragged over my head in a tangle of lace and elastic—"and kiss every single inch of skin"—he hooks his fingers beneath the waistband of my panties and pulls them down—"and lick until you know it's all mine."

Completely bare, with my hair tangled around my head after being rolled this way and that when he stripped me naked, I lie on the bed with my knees bent, my thighs pressed shyly together, and a blush heating my face. I desperately resist the urge to cover my breasts with my hands when he simply stands there with my panties dangling from his fingers, staring at me.

His voice is thick with arousal as he says, "I've never seen all of you before."

Because we've always been in semi-public places before. Cars, conference rooms, gardens. My blush deepens. "You've seen the parts that count."

"All of it counts." Stark hunger lines his face as his visual journey reaches the shadowed triangle between my thighs. He steps forward but I quickly scramble onto my knees, bracing my hand against his chest and bringing him to a halt.

"Not so fast, Your Majesty," I tell him, flicking open a button at his throat. "It's my turn."

Unlike him, I intend to take my time, savoring every hardened muscle and stretch of skin that I reveal. Slowly my fingers slide down to the second button.

Before I can unfasten it, they all suddenly   go flying when Maximilian tears his shirt open. He tosses it aside, then the vicious rip of his zipper joins the clatter of falling buttons.

"'Your Majesty' again?" His voice is low and silky, a tone that I've never heard from him before but sends delicious prickles of awareness racing across my skin. As if there's a dangerous predator standing in front of me… but I want to be eaten.

And he was right about all of it counting. Because I've seen parts of him during those long scenic drives. I've run my hands down the torso packed with muscle. I've licked the corrugated ridges of his abdomen. And I've seen his cock, stroked the thick curving length and sipped pearly beads of cum from the broad crown.

But completely naked, he's something else altogether. A temple of sculpted strength and power, with thighs like stone pillars and shoulders broad enough to support the sky.

My gaze settles on the colossal rise of his cock. Desire pools between my legs, and I'm pierced by a deep, empty ache as I imagine taking that massive length inside me. But first, I need to lick and claim. Moistening my lips, I reach for him.

Maximilian snags my wrists. My gaze flies up to meet his and encounter that dangerously predatory, heavy-lidded stare. "Taking your turn again?"

"Yes," I reply breathlessly. Trying to.

"And a king might let you have one." Hauling me forward by my wrists, he wraps his other arm around my waist. "But wanting you has turned me into a selfish bastard."

I gasp as I'm shoved backward—not hard, but with enough force to make me lose my balance. My shoulders hit the mattress, and in the next second I'm pinned to the bed with Maximilian above me. His left hand clamps my wrists together again and pushes them up and over my head. He kneels between my thighs, forcing them wide apart, and leans over with his big body braced above mine. His immense cock juts out between us, angling downward as if burdened by its own weight, the broad tip almost touching my lower belly.

For a long moment, his eyes simply devour the sight of me splayed helplessly beneath him. With my arms locked over my head, I can't look down at myself but I know what he must see, because every inch of my skin is alight, every sensation pitched at an acute intensity. My face is flushed, my lips parted and swollen. My every breath heaves an ocean of air through my chest, my full breasts swaying to the stormy rhythm, my nipples standing taut and proud.

A groan rumbles from his chest as his gaze settles between my legs. Exposed by the wide spread of my thighs, my most intimate flesh is completely revealed to him.

"Look at you, so wet and ready beneath me. And all fucking *mine*," he says, all the silk gone from his voice, replaced by gravel, and I shudder as his big hand possessively cups my pussy. His roughened fingers begin stroking through the drenched folds. "I'm going to make this sweet little cunt as hot and slick as it needs to be in order to take every inch of my cock. Because you're so fucking *tight*," he grits out and two of his long fingers push deep.

I cry out, my back arching as the hollow, empty ache inside me narrows into a sharp twinge of pain. My inner muscles clench hard, as if resisting the intrusion, then his thumb begins rubbing over my clit and the pain slides away into another ache, one that's deep and full and delicious.

"Just like that, Victoria. Christ, you're so damn beautiful." Regret and arousal roughen the words, but the kiss that follows is a gentle caress against my lips. "And I hate hurting you. But just this one time."

"I know." I pant my reply, still adjusting to the thrill of having part of him inside me, then catch my breath when his fingers begin slowly thrusting.

His gaze locked on my face, he studies my reaction. "Tell me when it starts feeling good."

"It's not *bad*," I gasp. I don't know what it is yet. It hurts and it doesn't, feels pleasurable and it doesn't.

"Not bad isn't the same as good." His thumb rolls over my clit, and his eyes narrow with satisfaction when I suck in a shuddering breath, seeking that same touch with a rock of my hips. "And *good* is only barely there. I want your pussy begging for it. I want you coming so hard that you'll be soft and slippery enough to take my cock without me hurting you again. Maybe you'll have to come a few times."

That hurt is only a dull memory now, and the tension inside me keeps shifting and changing with every thrust of his hand and circle of his thumb. He appears to be in more pain than I am. I can see the strain that holding back has put on him, stark need carving sharp lines into his angular features.

All to make certain I enjoy this. On a ragged little laugh, I say, "Tell me again how selfish you are?"

A soft growl rumbles from him. "You want me to start with the way I've got you laid out with your pussy open for the taking, and my hand pinning you down? All so I can fuck you good and hard. But this first time for us, I ought to be soft and slow and laying you on rose petals."

I shake my head, whimpering in frustration as he withdraws his fingers and begins gliding them through my folds again. Teasing. "Deciding what's best for me again? Because I don't want petals."

"And that's what I'm telling you. This isn't about what you want." His voice is harsh as his fingers dip inside me again. "I want to feel your pussy stretch around me as you take me in. I want you wet enough that it'll be the hottest fucking slide that I can imagine. Maybe it won't be an easy slide, with you so goddamn tight. But that's all right. I'll just fight my way in with you squirming beneath me like you are now."

Squirming because it's all changed. Because his voice is filling me up even deeper than his fingers are, and I can imagine all of it. "It feels good now," I pant. "It's feeling so good."

"You think I can't hear that is? And feel it? You were wet before but now you're soaked." Another rough groan escapes him as he strokes through my drenched heat, and I can hear it, too, even over the pounding of my heart. "That's so I can get in you balls-deep and know those sweet juices are slicking up every inch of my cock. Though maybe I'll have to get you on your hands and knees before I can get that deep."

Oh god. I bite my lip against a scream of frustration when he abandons my clit to tease his fingers through my swollen folds, gliding over all that wetness. Desperate for more, to touch myself if I have to, I try to tug my arms out of his grip, but the hand pinning my wrists only tightens.

"I pictured you on your knees so many times, Victoria.

Ever since that photo of you in that ski suit. All I could think of is getting you bare and fucking into you from behind. Sometimes with you pushing back at me with your greedy cunt trying to take as much of my cock as it can, sometimes with me holding you still so I can ride you so fucking hard."

"*So* hard," I echo on desperate little sob, writhing against his teasing fingers.

"Your pussy wants to be filled up now, doesn't it?"

"*Please.*"

I cry out when his fingers push into me, each slow thrust gently caressing my sensitive inner walls, but it's the new, firmer stroke over my clit that begins shoving me toward the brink. Back bowing up off the bed, I struggle for breath, for sense, but only find his voice urging me on.

"Christ, look at you. You'll be under me just like this, Victoria, except it'll be my cock pumping so deep into you and making you come. *Fuck,* and your pussy's just getting tighter, pulling me in." His mouth hovers over mine, as if ready to capture the ecstasy that's threatening to erupt on my every gasping moan. "I bet your pussy will suck up all my cum, too. Because when I get into you, Victoria, there's nothing that'll get me out before I'm done. I'll fill you with so much cum that I'll be overflowing your cunt when I'm—"

He breaks off when my inner muscles clench hard, then groans like a tortured man. "*This* is what I wanted."

For me to come. And the orgasm tears through me

like an avalanche, starting with my pussy clamping down on his fingers, then ecstasy breaking free in a tumbling rush, picking up speed and sensation as it roars past every quaking muscle, the devastation barely contained within my skin. I'm crushed beneath it, then abruptly flung out across a precipice.

His kiss catches me on the way down, gentler than I expect, because I can still feel the taut restraint holding his aroused body in check. But he doesn't move to fill me up with his cock, though he has to be in agony and my body is more than ready for him now.

Instead he lifts his head and looks down at me, his eyes still burning and his voice like gravel. As he speaks, his wet fingers glide upward and over my belly, my stomach muscles quivering in their wake, then trace a slow circle around my navel. "When you imagined your role as queen, did you want children right away or want to wait? Your preference will also become mine."

Taken aback by the unexpectedness of the question, a moment passes before I realize the full import of what he just offered. He's consulting me, and letting me choose the kind of queen I will be...?

Just as he promised.

My heart nearly bursts with love for him, followed by a surge of heat as I realize *why* he's asking. Boldly I tell him, "I want you to fill me up with cum, Your Majesty."

"I will," he says gruffly, but doesn't. Instead he finally releases my hands to cup my jaw and tenderly stroke his thumb across my lips. "I will never let you go, Victoria. And if you ever run away, there's nowhere in the world that I won't follow."

A wistful little smile curves my mouth. Because that's lovely, but… "In twelve years, you never even went twenty miles to Gentian."

Regret shadows his eyes. "And you deserved better. But that was then. And now I travel twice that distance just to be alone with you for forty minutes."

Wonder fills me. "Is that why you went to Vespa with me?"

"It wasn't for the chicken dinner. What did you think was my reason for going?"

So that we could pretend to be a loving couple. But I don't want to think about that part of our engagement now.

"No." His eyes darken dangerously, and suddenly my arms are pinned again. Maximilian looms over me, his jaw clenched. "There it is again. You're running away."

I'm not even moving. "What?"

"*Fuck.*" Frustration boils off him—but agony lurks in his gaze and desolation edges the steel of his voice. "I know you've been hurting. I thought it must have been this thing about whether you'll just be a breeder or a queen, and not being sure about marrying me. But we resolved that. So I didn't think I'd see this look on your face again. So what is it? Tell me what's making you so unhappy, and I'll fix it."

My heart aching, I turn my head to escape that desperate,

searching gaze. I'm almost ashamed by the answer he's seeking. For so long, the only thing I wanted was to marry Maximilian. And now I've been given everything I wanted, but I'm still unhappy and hurting.

Either I'm the world's most ungrateful bitch…or I didn't know *what* I really wanted. Because I told myself that I didn't expect Maximilian to love me, but it still ripped me apart when it was only pretend. So I *do* want his love.

But I can't ask for that. He would try to give me anything I wished for, but love can't be granted with a wish. And he hasn't had time to fall in love with me.

Yet.

That realization slips through me like a healing balm. He hasn't had time to fall in love…*yet*. But we have mutual respect and admiration. Shared obligations and duties and interests. Explosive sexual attraction.

So I just need to do what I have always done: work toward a goal, and wait for him. But this time the goal won't be marrying him or becoming a queen. Instead I want to win his heart. Maybe it'll take months, or even years. But his love would be worth the wait.

As long as it's not fake. Because when it is, it tears me apart.

"There is one thing you can do," I finally tell him, my voice thick. "Don't pretend to love me anymore."

Despite my calm resolution and my certainty that I'll eventually gain his love, it's still difficult to meet his gaze—fearing he'll see the pain inside of me and know how vulnerable not having his heart makes me.

But instead of pity, I only see a dark frown laced with confusion, as if he didn't understand what I said.

"You don't want me to pretend anymore?" Now disbelief joins the puzzlement.

Probably because I was the one who suggested that tactic in the first place. Throat aching, I nod. "I know we agreed to, for Kapria's sake. But when we're in public, you should only be as you really are. We are friends enough by now, I think, that no one could see the difference between fake love and real companionship."

His eyes narrow. His big body bends closer to mine, and he grips his thick cock at the base. Drawing back, he angles his shaft and drags the broad crown the length of my slit, parting my swollen pussy lips and gliding his cockhead up and down my acutely sensitized flesh.

Over the sound of my needy moan, he asks silkily, "We are *friends*?"

"With benefits!" I gasp, shuddering with pleasure and need before adding breathlessly, "Which will make it even harder for anyone watching us to tell the difference. But *we* will know. And it won't…" I trail off on a ragged breath, closing my eyes before forcing out the rest in a strained whisper. "It won't hurt anymore."

Instantly he stops the teasing caress of his cock. "Victoria."

My name is a quiet demand to meet his gaze. No

puzzlement or disbelief clouds his expression now, his dark eyes clear and direct.

"I have *never* pretended to love you. In public and private, everything I've said and done with you was because I truly felt it. Everything I said in that interview was true, too. I saw you at your house and by the time we arrived at the palace, I knew."

The painful ache within me softens, my love for him drawing out all the poison that had been seeping into my soul ever since we'd agreed to pretend for the cameras.

"You don't have to pretend now, either," I tell him gently, though I understand why he did. He doesn't want to see me hurt and wants to find a way to fix it. "It's sweet and generous, but unnecessary."

As if taken aback, he stares down at me for a long second. "You don't believe that I love you?"

"It's too fast to believe. You didn't even know me."

He scowls, his expression darkening. "And you fell in love during a speech. Yet you don't say that was too fast. Neither did Andrew Bush."

"Because twelve years have passed, which proves that it is steady and true. But in that same time, millions of other teenage girls fell in love and out again. If not for the betrothal, without the hope that kept my love alive, I might have moved on, too." Though I'm not certain I could have ever completely moved on; he would have always owned a part of my heart. "And you must know that what I feel now isn't the same as I did then. The more I learned of you, the more my love has changed and grown. That girl's love is a mere spark compared to what I feel now."

"What I know is that I'm not a teenage girl. And what I feel is a hell of a lot more than a *spark*." He snarls the word and that dangerous light enters his gaze again. "I'll prove it to you, then. Even if it takes me twelve fucking years to do it."

He surges forward, plunging the full length of his cock into me—then holds himself deep, so incredibly deep, our bodies locked together and utterly still. My mind reeling with shock and pleasure, I'm arched in a tight bow beneath him, my pussy desperately clenching around that thick shaft as I struggle to adjust to his massive size. There's no pain, only unyielding pressure as my interior walls are stretched to the limit and scorched by the heat of his erection.

Above me, Maximilian's powerful body is like a sculpture, his every muscle a stone carved in sharp relief. His dark eyes are glazed over and unseeing, as if the same shock and pleasure that paralyzed me still holds him in its luscious grip.

Then a shudder wracks his body. The echo of that quake inside me sends a spasm of greedy lust through my inner muscles. A choked cry fills my throat as my pussy clutches his cock even tighter, and Maximilian groans, a deep and tortured sound that rumbles from his chest.

The glassy sheen in his eyes begins to clear and he

looks down at me, his voice a thick rasp. "I knew that being inside you would feel amazing. But I didn't know that you'd feel *this* fucking amazing. Better than anything I imagined."

A tremulous laugh ripples through me. "I think it's *you* who feels amazing inside *me*."

His gaze sharpens into a determined gleam. "Or it's because I love you."

The words steal my breath, then his body steals every response as he moves, drawing back and leaving an empty burning ache before driving into me again. Another cry escapes me, then his mouth finds mine in a hot, open kiss. I don't know when he let go of my wrists but I can't stop touching him, clutching at his shoulders, spearing my fingers into his short hair. His big hand grips my ass and he angles my hips upward, and the next stroke is even deeper when he fucks back into me—then again, and again, setting a hard rhythm that sends me spiraling toward mindless ecstasy, my entire world narrowing to Maximilian and the feel of his thick cock pumping relentlessly into the slick, tightening grip of my pussy.

Then he slows…and slows. I frantically urge him faster again, but he lifts his head and, with one strong hand gripping my hip and preventing me from rocking up against him, begins to stroke the full length of his cock into me, each thrust an excruciatingly endless glide from base of his shaft to the bulging crown.

It's exquisite torture for me—and for him. Tension

shakes through his entire body, tendons straining. Sweat beads over his skin and runs in rivulets down ridges of muscle.

"Look at me, Victoria." His eyes are burning coals, his voice resonating from the depths of his broad chest, as if there was a hollow space beneath his heart that housed both agony and hope. "Can't you see that I love you?"

Sheer joy and wonder overfill my heart, clogging my throat. Because there's no pretense here. His emotions lay exposed, as naked as our bodies. And I know what's blazing out at me.

I see that he's in love with me.

On a muffled sob, I reach for him. His kiss is a revelation now, full of all the love that I couldn't sense before. I don't know how or why he fell so quickly, but it's everything I ever wanted—and better than I dreamed.

His mouth devours mine as he begins thrusting faster into me, my body and heart caught in a maelstrom of exultation and pleasure. And when I began to come, I don't know if the ecstasy that crashes through my body really is so much deeper and sharper than before—or if my heart is so much bigger now that my entire being feels every sensation so much more intensely.

Or maybe I come harder simply because he loves me.

Crying out his name, I cling to my king as my paroxysms of pleasure squeeze the thick shaft inside me—and hold him closer as he hunches over with another tortured groan, pounding deeper, his strokes suddenly erratic. His mouth is open and hot against mine, his chest a bellows dragging in ragged heaving breaths. Strong fingers digging into my soft thigh, he shoves my knee higher, opening my legs wider and grinding against the sopping wetness of my pussy until he's in me so deep that there can't be any more of my cunt to claim.

Abruptly he throws back his head, jaw clenched, and seems locked in an epic struggle against his own body, his torso utterly rigid and unmoving, his knees planted against the mattress and the flex of his thighs and buttocks continuing to pump his cock in and out of my heated depths. Then a violent quake hits him and inside me his cock feels bigger now, hotter, and with a groan of defeat he goes utterly still. His mouth captures mine as he comes, thrusting shallowly as his shaft pulses against my inner walls.

With a laughing groan, he buries his face against my neck. "Your pussy's *too* amazing, especially when you come. I couldn't hold out."

I laugh, sliding my hands over his sweat-slicked shoulders. "Next time."

"Which will be very soon." Maximilian punctuates that promise with a rock of his hips that leaves me gasping with sweet pleasure. Then he lifts his head and tenderly kisses my mouth. "If your pussy is up to it."

"Maybe a warm bath first," I say softly. "And I love you."

"So you believe I'm not pretending?" His voice is gruff.

I cup his face in my hands. "I believe it."

"Good." This time his kiss is swift and hard. "But I'll still keep fucking your doubts away."

I laugh, delighted by the idea. "You can fuck them away whenever you like, Your Majesty. But before you do…" My hand slips between us to curl around his cock, still erect and glistening with our cum. "…can I finally have my turn, or are you still feeling selfish? Because I want to stake a claim with my tongue."

And this time, the king wasn't feeling selfish at all.

Maximilian

I fuck Victoria's doubts away throughout that afternoon, the next week, and the next month. She claims not a single doubt remains, not since that first time. But I won't take any chances. We barely get enough time together to show her how much I love her, so I take my opportunities where I can, and if that means keeping her body overwhelmed by her need for me, I'll do it. Because losing her would fucking destroy me, and I won't feel secure until she's bound to me in marriage—and standing beside me as my queen.

But I also know damn well that doesn't always count for anything. My mother was a queen, married to a king whom she loved…and the cruel bastard fucked everything up, hurting her so bad that she couldn't bear to stay.

I won't *ever* do that to Victoria.

…except I did, for twelve years. Not deliberately. But making her feel like an invisible *nothing* all the same.

She's forgiven me for it, I know. To her the past is done with; all that matters is our future. But the way she looked at me with tears swimming in her eyes, all that anger and pain bursting out of her like a festering boil, is something I'll never forget. And I never *should* forget it. With my carelessness, I wounded her heart—and carelessness is a passive, inactive thing, but it can still harm. Caring means making the effort. Even if that effort is simply being mindful of what I say and do for her…and being mindful of what I don't do and say to her.

That's a vow I make long before our wedding day.

That morning arrives after the longest fucking night I've known in a while. And despite all the reasons that the ceremony, the procession from the chapel to the palace, and the wedding reception afterward is important—despite all that it symbolizes to the citizens of my kingdom and helps raise Kapria's profile around the world—every selfish part of me just wants it to be over. I want to skip to the part where Victoria's mine, and she's sleeping beside me every night.

But I contain my impatience as I'm pressed and polished and buffed from my head to my toes. Across the city, in a hotel suite on a floor reserved solely for the bride and her bridal party, Victoria's likely undergoing a much more complicated ordeal. The wedding ceremony begins at noon—an hour away—and I'm just now dressing for it, whereas her first stylist was scheduled to arrive at seven in the morning.

Nearby, I see Geoffrey check his phone. "Still on schedule?"

He and Ursula have been in constant contact, so that if there's any delay we'll immediately be able to adjust our timeline.

But with no hiccups, in ten minutes I'll leave the palace on foot. The church is only a twenty minute walk away, in the southwest corner of the royal grounds. Around the same time that I arrive at the chapel, Victoria's car will begin the drive across the city, and it's all coordinated so that she arrives at the chapel's front steps immediately before noon.

And why the fuck is it taking him so long to answer? A knot of tension twists in my gut. "Geoffrey!" I bark. "Are they still on schedule?"

"Yes, Your Majesty," he confirms. "Still on schedule."

The tension doesn't completely release. I scowl at him and he gives me a bland look. "I had to wait for Ursula's reply, Your Majesty."

I hate waiting. For anything. I don't know how Victoria waited so long for me, except that she's the most perfect being ever created.

With the most perfect cunt. Sweet and hot and when

I get her alone again, it will belong to a queen. Whenever her pussy gets so damn slick and greedy, she won't need to beg anymore. She'll just command me to taste it, to fuck it. And I'll serve at her whim.

That thought helps get me through the next ten minutes, which each seem like an eternity determined to keep me away from her. Finally it's time to go. I glance at Geoffrey. I don't even need to ask.

"Still on schedule," he says.

Anticipation fills my chest. "Notify Karl," I tell him. The palace grounds are open to the public today so all of Kapria can celebrate in the wedding. Enormous tents are set up on the lawns, offering refreshments and, after the wedding ceremony is over, champagne and cake. Even now, though the walls of the palace, I can hear the large gathering crowd. My path to the chapel has been kept clear—not out of fear of an attack, but simply to make certain I'm not delayed—but as soon as I start my walk, Karl's security team will discreetly secure every step of the way.

But the man himself will be walking with me, and serving as my best man.

Tilting his head toward the chamber door, Geoffrey says, "He's here."

In a Kaprian uniform that manages to destroy the image of a nondescript man, and instead revealing the deadly force that he truly is. But he's not alone. Philippa's with him, dressed for the wedding in a pantsuit and boxy hat perched atop her gray hair. I stride over to greet her, hoping like hell that she doesn't intend to make the walk with us. Under any other circumstances, I'd be happy to have her along. She's a fine advisor and a good friend… but her walk is slow as hell.

I take her outstretched hand and kiss her cheeks. "I am set to leave now. Geoffrey will arrange a car to take you to the chapel. Have you seen my mother yet?"

She's long been a friend of my mother's, and one of the few supporting figures that had stood up to my father during those worst years.

"We had breakfast together this morning."

As Victoria and I did, yesterday morning. And there my bride once again proved how perfect she is, because I hadn't expected it to be as awkward as it was. I have no hard feelings toward my mother. No resentments. She'd been right to leave my father. Hell, I'd even *told* her to go. And speaking to her over the years has never been anything but easy—but those conversations had also always been short and infrequent.

So that might be why I had so little to say when we were finally face-to-face. But Victoria took over the conversation so easily and naturally, keeping my mother engaged with questions about her new family—and making it seem as if I was the source of many of those questions. As if I'd spoken to Victoria about my mother many, many times. And I don't know if my mother even recognized that she'd done it.

In the car afterward, she simply climbed into my lap and tucked her head against my shoulder, letting me hold her. And she didn't say a word, but she didn't have to. I don't resent my mother. But her leaving left its quiet mark on me, somehow. Or maybe it wasn't her leaving, but not taking me with her. Rationally, I know it would have been impossible to fight my father. But I don't know if the young boy I was truly believed or understood that when I told her to go. Which is probably the same part of me that's always so fucking worried that Victoria won't stay.

But Victoria didn't say that either. She didn't have to. We both know.

Karl clears his throat. Time to head out. Then Philippa's hands tighten on mine—and I realize that his prompt wasn't for me, but for her.

"I came to offer my sincere congratulations on your wedding," she tells me in a wavering voice. "But also to beg your forgiveness."

I frown, then realization hits me square in the chest. "You leaked that meeting?"

The one that is *still* the reason a few tabloids like to put 'horrible' in front of Victoria's name. Not all the time. Not even most of the time. But it stuck.

She nods, her lips quivering.

"Why?" I demand. "You wanted me to marry a banker's daughter that much?"

"Not Felicity, necessarily. Just someone who wasn't a duty and obligation. You never took anything for yourself,

Maximilian. And then you intended to marry this girl who'd been nothing to you and—who I believed would continue to be nothing."

"So you made that decision without consulting me?" And I understand why Victoria had been so angry when I'd done the same to her. Even the best intentions are worth shit when a choice is taken away.

Regret darkens her eyes. "I was wrong. And I saw how wrong I was almost immediately. When I saw you with her, and saw that you were finally taking something for yourself, I realized the woman I believed would be a problem was a solution. And that you loved her. So when that horrible article did not seem to affect your relationship *with* her, I was relieved. I contacted the tabloid journalist and told him not to use anything more of what I'd given him regarding that meeting. And since there was nothing else, I'd hoped that would be the end of it."

Dread fills my chest. "But it wasn't?"

"There was more today. So I called the tabloid and ordered them to rescind it, because I'd retracted my permission to use anything more, but of course that was nothing. But that phone call apparently tipped off Mr. Sauer."

Karl. Who's waiting now for me to decide what to do about Philippa…and to walk with me to the chapel.

I don't have any fucking time for this. "I leave for my honeymoon tomorrow. I expect to find your resignation when I return. You'll cite a desire to retire."

Eyes wavering but her mouth firm, accepting that punishment, Philippa nods.

To Karl, I say, "Let's go. Geoffrey? Walk with us." Which wasn't the original plan but I don't give a fuck. They fall into step beside me and I ask him, "Did you find it?"

"Here it is." He hands over a tablet, the screen already open to the website.

A Royal Sham—Or A Horrible Trap?

Did King Max make a devil's bargain to save his kingdom? Sources close to King Max reveal that despite public appearances that suggest a love match, his marriage to socialite Victoria Dietrich is the result of a longstanding betrothal agreement between the power-hungry billionaire and the impoverished king. But the royal hunk was apparently so reluctant to marry his horrible bride, that he delayed for twelve years before resigning himself to his fate. 'He doesn't even love the girl,' a source claimed—and noted that when his advisors pointed out that he was being forced to marry a girl he didn't love, King Max admitted that he didn't even know her.

This is contrary to how the couple behave at public appearances. Never has a king and his future queen seemed more in love. But is it all pretend?

"It's bullshit," Karl dismisses.

So it is. Mostly true. But all bullshit.

Yet a sour ball of worry lodged itself in my throat anyway. Because if Victoria saw this…how could it *not* hurt her? Because she'll know it's bullshit, too. But she'll also know that it's mostly true. Or was. But simply being reminded might bring back all those doubts that I've worked so goddamn hard to erase.

If she's seen it. She's been busy with her stylists all morning. But I've seen her ask Ursula to read out loud the news headlines or emails while having her hair styled before.

"Find out if Victoria has seen it," I tell Geoffrey.

Then we exit the palace and there's no use to try and continue talking. As soon as I step into sight, the crowd begins cheering. And this is what matters. Not the tabloid gossip. But seeing so many Kaprians happy. That has been my only purpose for so long. And with Victoria's help, we'll do even more than I did before.

Though I want to reach the church as quickly as possible, this is important, too. So I slow my pace and wave for their personal photos, shaking hands where I can, accepting flowers from little girls here and there. I reach the chapel after my scheduled time but it doesn't matter much—she's not here yet, and isn't supposed to be for at least thirty minutes.

I look to Geoffrey the second we get inside. "Well?"

"She hadn't seen it—"

I scowl. "Hadn't?"

Geoffrey grimaces. "Not until I asked Ursula if she had, and piqued their interest."

My chest tightens. So she *wouldn't* have seen it. But now she has. And less than an hour before our wedding, when any doubts she might already have must be gnawing away at her.

"Has the car left the hotel?" It should be leaving now.
"I'll find out."

But not before I'm greeted by the archbishop. The
next twenty minutes is fucking torture as I accompany
him to his chambers and I sign what I need to sign and
sit through his blessing, but my only prayer is that she's
on her way.

When I emerge from the chambers, I search for Geoffrey but only find Karl. "Is she on the way?"

"No." He shrugs. "There was a delay."

Tight bands wrap around my chest, making it hard
to breathe. "What kind of delay?"

"My people don't know. Just that there is one." He
frowns at me. "It's usual for weddings."

Not royal ones. Fuck.

I find Geoffrey in the crowded church hall. A thousand
guests will fill the pews today. As soon as he sees my face,
he rushes to say, "They're on their way, Your Majesty."

Relief eases constriction around my heart. "What
was the delay?"

"Ursula wouldn't say."

What the hell? That worries me more than any other
answer could. Because there's no reason that couldn't be
said. Her makeup's not done, a button on her dress broke,
a stuck elevator—there's nothing to hide.

The only thing a bride or her assistant might want
to conceal is that, for a short time, Victoria didn't want

to come. "Tell Ursula that it's by the king's command. I demand to know."

He looks abashed. "I tried that already. She shut me down. And said that she was following the queen's orders."

Even if she's not yet the queen, I won't start off our marriage by undermining her in front of our staff. So there's nothing to do but wait and ask her myself.

The next half hour is the longest of my life. I picture Victoria in her hotel suite, assailed by doubts before bolstering her courage and deciding to come. I picture her in the car, still doubting and ordering the driver to head for the airport, instead. I picture her arriving at the front steps of the church, looking up and seeing a future she doesn't want anymore, then racing away.

I'll chase after her if she does. I told her before. There's nowhere I won't follow.

But I don't have to go anywhere. I just have to stand before the altar, my heart pounding and swelling with the music from the organ that announces her arrival.

Liz comes through the doors first, holding a sprig of wildflowers. She walks down the aisle with mincing steps, and another eternity passes before Victoria's sister finally stands at the front of the church. Then everyone rises to their feet.

And I was so fucking wrong about wanting to skip ahead past the ceremony. To skip past the moment she appears at the end of the aisle, a vision in white framed by the ornate archway that leads to the antechamber. A thousand eyes are turned in her direction, but she's not looking at any of them. Instead her gaze is fixed on me, the happy tears shining in her eyes turning them into a sapphire sea.

Her brother is giving her away, but I'm barely aware of James at her side. I spend every moment memorizing her appearance, from the tiara nestled in her thick dark hair to the embroidered lace that cups her breasts and cinches at her waist, to the flaring skirt and the long train that trails behind her. All of it, I commit to memory. Her hands, trembling slightly as they hold her bouquet. Her lips, curved into a smile that I want to spend a lifetime kissing.

And her feet, because I know that every single step they take is a decision she makes—and every step is bringing her to me.

I don't know how much time passes before she reaches my side. It seems an instant, not long enough to memorize every detail of how she looks on the day she gives herself to me. It seems an eternity, an endless delay before I can make her mine. But it doesn't matter either way.

For Victoria, I would have waited forever.

But I won't wait to take away any pain she might be feeling. "What was the delay?" I murmur as she abandons James's escort to take my arm, and I lead her up the steps to the dais where the archbishop waits.

She muffles a giggle and shakes her head, whispering, "Nothing."

I know that's not true. "You saw the article."

"I did." Her gaze is slyly amused—not wary or pained as it used to be in the days when she would run from me, and I let myself relax slightly.

"It was bullshit. I love you. I'll *always* love you."

"And I love you," she responds softly, then slants a laughing glance at me. "You shouldn't believe everything you read in those rags, Your Majesty. Even if it's mostly true."

Fair enough. "Then what was the delay?"

She grimaces slightly. "I threw up."

"You were sick?" Desperately I search her face. She doesn't look ill. "Did you have second thoughts? Or were nerves to blame?"

"I suspect your cum was to blame," she whispers quickly, then we halt in front of the archbishop.

And maybe I do want to skip ahead. Because as soon as I realize what she implied, I pull Victoria into my arms—and get to the part where I'm kissing the bride.

Epilogue

One year later...

*I've always been an impatient bastard. I prob-*ably always will be. I hate wasting even a minute doing nothing.

For a long time, Victoria was the only exception to that. With her, there's nothing wasted about a minute spent in her company, even if all we do lie on a beach for a month, as we did for our honeymoon. Or spending a lazy Sunday morning in bed—even if we're not fucking, though usually plenty of that takes up the time, too.

But now I've got another exception. And not a moment spent with baby Wilhelm is a wasted moment. Not the hours simply holding him, or letting him cling to my big finger while he gurgles up at me, or walking the floor with Wilhelm on my shoulder while Victoria sleeps—as I am now. We've got nannies and nurses who can do it all, but when it comes to Wilhelm, the only wasted moments are the moments that I *could* spend with him but don't. So I make the effort to do as much as my other duties and obligations allow. And with Victoria sharing those duties and obligations, we both have more time—for each other and our son.

When he's finally asleep, I return him to his crib. Moonlight filters through the drapes in my bedchamber and falls across the bed, where Victoria lies in a tangle of sheets. Not sleeping any longer, I realize as I slip into the bed and she turns toward me.

"Diaper?" she says drowsily.

"Diaper," I confirm, wrapping my arms around her.

She sighs and snuggles in closer, just as naked as the way I left her. "What was wrong with your face in the garden today?"

"My face? Nothing." Bemused, I tilt my head against the pillow to gaze down her. "Why?"

"Because right after we were playing in the garden with him today, you poked at your cheeks…like when you poke at something to see if it's sore. It was strange. And I just remembered it."

I do, too, and have to laugh. "Because I realized they didn't ache."

She comes up on her elbow, and for a moment I'm distracted by the sway of her breasts—even fuller and rounder than before her pregnancy, and her nipples more pronounced.

"Why would your cheeks ache?"

"From too much smiling."Tempted beyond resistance, I push her onto her back and lower my head to her breast. "But apparently in the past year, my cheeks have gotten more exercise. Because I spent hours with you and Wilhelm, smiling the whole time, and they didn't hurt after."

"You do smile more," she agrees with a gasp, clutching at my hair as I circle my tongue around the rosy peak, loving the way it stiffens, as if standing and begging for more. "But that's not the only exercise your mouth has been getting this past year."

I shout with laughter, then rise up to kiss her. She giggles against my lips, then adds, "My jaw still aches every time, though. So maybe if you let me have a turn more often, I could get more exercise, too."

I kiss that lovely jaw. "You get plenty of turns, my queen.The only issue there is that your mouth is too small."

"You always say my mouth is perfect," she retorts.

"Then my cock must be too big. I'll accept that as a flaw."I kiss her when she laughs again, then kiss her more slowly, until her laughter dissolves into soft, breathless moans. And her mouth *is* perfect.The lush heat of it, her every laugh and smile.

Every part of her is perfect, and my mouth worships

it all, from the sensitive hollow behind her ears to her delicate little feet that always bring her back to me. And her cunt, her sweet delicious cunt—it's utterly perfect, juicy and hot beneath my tongue, then so fucking tight around my cock as I push inside her.

She cries out, clinging to me with her hands on my shoulders and her ankles linked behind my back and her pussy holding me in its exquisite grip. And as I slowly fuck her, driving us both to the shattering finish, the most pleasure her perfect mouth gives me isn't the smiling or the kissing or the licking—it's the "I love you" that she whispers at the end.

Printed in Great Britain
by Amazon

2 4 DEC 2021